Uncle from Another Planet

D1446954

#4

Uncle from Another Planet

Paul Buchanan
Created by Paul Buchanan and Rod Randall

BROADMAN
& HOLMAN
PUBLISHERS
Nashville, Tennessee

0-8054-1650-1

Published by Broadman & Holman Publishers,
Nashville, Tennessee
Editorial Team: Vicki Crumpton, Janis Whipple, Kim Overcash
Typesetting: SL Editorial Services

Dewey Decimal Classification: Fiction
Subject Heading: UNIDENTIFIED FLYING OBJECTS—FICTION /
CHRISTIAN LIFE—FICTION
Library of Congress Card Catalog Number: 98-37533

All Scripture citation is from the King James Version.

Library of Congress Cataloging-in-Publication Data

Buchanan, Paul, 1959–
    Uncle from another planet / by Paul Buchanan.
        p.   cm. — (Heebie Jeebies : #4)
    Summary: Eleven-year-old Ryan wonders how he can take
his problems to God when his stay at his great-uncle's iso-
lated farm brings him in contact with a flying saucer and
the possibility of being abducted by aliens.
    ISBN 0-8054-1650-1 (pbk.)
    [1. Unidentified flying objects—Fiction. 2. Extraterrestrial
beings—Fiction. 3. Great-uncles—Fiction. 4. Christian
life—Fiction. 5. Horror stories.] I. Title. II. Series:
Heebie Jeebies series : v. 4
PZ7.B87717Un   1999
[Fic]—dc21

                                                      98-37533
                                                          CIP
                                                           AC

1 2 3 4 5   03 02 01 00 99

DEDICATION

For Uncle Javez

Chapter 1

Yesterday morning, Saturday, I didn't even know I *had* an Uncle Allen, and today I was on my way to his farm to stay for a week. I wasn't looking forward to spending a week with a complete stranger, but at least my brother, Jeremy, and my cousin, Angie, were coming with me.

"We need some gas," Mom said from the driver's seat of our Jeep Cherokee. Her voice was bright and cheery. "Why don't we stop at the next town? We can all get out for a stretch. Maybe they'll have a Coke machine." I could tell Mom was trying to sound enthusiastic to cheer us up.

We'd been driving for about three hours now. The trip was interesting at first—when we were going over the mountains—but as we came down on the other side, I could see the freeway stretching in front of us in a perfectly straight line across endless flat farmland.

We drove on the straight freeway a while and then got off on a country highway—also perfectly straight. Pretty soon the roads we passed didn't have names anymore; they just had numbers: Route 117, Route 247—that sort of thing.

For the last hour every boring mile of road looked exactly like the last—the same fields, the same barns, the same telephone poles. It was almost like we were standing still.

I looked up in the front seat at Jeremy. He is three years older than I am, almost fifteen. He's a pretty cool brother most of the time, but he still treats me like a little kid. Jeremy was looking out the window at all the fields going by as we breezed along the empty highway. He yawned and scratched the back of his head.

Angie was in the back seat with me. She sat behind my mom. She was leaning back with her head resting on the back of the seat. Her eyes were closed, but I was pretty sure she wasn't sleeping. Angie is three months older than I am. We picked her up right after her family got home from church. They go to church a lot. I even noticed that she packed her Bible to come on this trip. She seems like she enjoys reading it. Our family has a Bible, too—somewhere—but I've never really looked at it.

My little brother, Dylan, sat in the back seat between Angie and me. He was just along for the ride, and he'd be riding back home with Mom once she dropped the rest of us off at Uncle Allen's. Dylan had a pad of paper propped on his knees. He'll start kindergarten when summer is over. Dylan loves to draw, and that's what he was doing now.

He was coloring a blue sky when he dropped his crayon again.

"Ryan," he said, tugging at the sleeve of my T-shirt. "Help."

"Stop dropping your crayons," I told him. "This is about the millionth time I've had to pick one up for you." I bent over and felt around on the floor at my feet until I found his stubby crayon. It felt sticky. I handed it to Dylan and wiped my hand on my shorts. Little kids—*sheesh*!

"You know you shouldn't be drawing while we're driving," I told him. "You're going to get carsick."

Dylan ignored me and began scribbling his blue sky again.

"If you feel like you're going to barf," I told him, "make sure you do it on Angie." Jeremy laughed and glanced over his shoulder at me. Angie stuck out her tongue without opening her eyes.

I looked down at the picture Dylan was drawing. "What *is* that?" I asked him. "Is that our house?"

He shook his head and kept scribbling over a solid patch of blue.

"Well what is it?" I asked him.

He pointed at the boxy shape I thought was a house. "This is the gas station," he told me.

"The one we stopped at when we went up the mountain?"

"No," he said. "The one we're going to now."

"Oh," I said, leaning closer to look at the drawing. In the middle of the picture was an oval, black splotch. "What's this here?" I asked him, tapping the black shape with my finger. "Some kind of oil slick?"

"No," he told me. "That's the big, black dog."

I tilted my head and studied the black blob on the paper. It *did* have four legs, now that he mentioned it. "What*ever*," I said.

Uncle Allen was really my mom's uncle, though she hadn't seen him in five or six years. She insisted that I'd met him before and that I'd been to his farm, but I couldn't remember that far back. I was only Dylan's age when our family had been there last. Jeremy claimed he remembered Uncle Allen well, but I thought he was pulling my leg.

This week, my parents were joining Angie's parents on a cruise, so the three of us were being dropped off at Uncle Allen's farm. Mom called everyone she knew last month, looking for someone to take care of us. Uncle Allen was the only one who could. Dylan gets to stay at my aunt's apartment in town, but she didn't have room for the rest of us.

Last night before we left, Mom called me to the kitchen table and showed me where Wellum was on the map. Wellum is the town closest to where Uncle Allen has his farm. Wellum wasn't actually *on* the map, but she made a little pencil mark where it would have been, had anyone at Rand McNally known it existed.

"You'll have the time of your life," she promised me. "It'll be an adventure. You'll be out of the city—out breathing the fresh air and running wild with Jeremy and Angie." She took a sip of coffee. I studied the map.

"Why isn't it on the map?" I asked her. "Don't they want to admit it's there?"

Mom ignored my question. "Uncle Allen has a goat and some chickens," she said enthusiastically. "He's got a barn and a tractor. You'll be close to nature. You can go bird watching."

"*Bird watching?*" I said. "I've already seen birds."

Mom laughed and mussed up my hair. I smiled back at her, even though I wasn't thrilled with the prospect of being shipped off to somebody's boring farm for a week of bird watching.

"Just try to be good," Mom warned me. "Uncle Allen isn't used to children. In fact he isn't used to having anyone around; he's been living on his own for thirty years. I'm afraid the three of you might be too much for him."

"We'll take it easy on him," I promised. "He'll still be alive when you come pick us up."

"I hope so," she said. "I hope you'll do everything he tells you and not get in his way too much. I'll be worrying about you all week."

"Sounds like maybe you should be worrying about Uncle Allen," I told her with a grin.

I looked out the window now at the passing fields. I understood why Wellum wasn't on the map. We'd been looking on the Fullman County map. We should have been looking on the Middle-of-Nowhere map.

"Here we go," Mom said. "Here's our stop."

I leaned forward and looked over Jeremy's shoulder out the front windshield. Sure enough, there was a little gas station up ahead at a cross-roads.

"Let's all get out and stretch our legs," Mom said with forced cheeriness.

Mom turned off the highway and onto the gravel lot. This wasn't anything like the gas stations we had back home in the city—with the rows of electronic pumps and the high, white roofs full of fluorescent lights. This was more like an old fix-it garage with a dented tow truck and a couple of ancient-looking gas pumps. It wasn't even paved.

"I think we've gone through some kind of time warp," I told Mom from the back seat. "If this were in black and white, I'd think we were in Mayberry."

Mom pulled in front of one of the pumps and cut the engine. She pulled out her purse and rummaged through it.

I opened my door and the dry summer heat rushed in, like I had opened an oven. I stepped down onto the gravel. My legs were stiff from sitting so long. I saw some movement over in the open garage. A man crawled out from under the pickup truck he'd been working on and walked toward us, wiping his hands on a red rag. He was wearing blue coveralls and a green John Deere cap. His hands and forearms were streaked black with grease.

Jeremy, Angie, and Dylan were all out of the car now. Dylan was jumping up and down to hear the gravel crunch under his feet. Jeremy walked over toward the garage.

"Here, Ryan," Mom said. I went around the back of the Jeep with its bike rack, to Mom's open window. She was holding out a handful of change she'd fished out of her purse. "Go see if they have a Coke machine." The mechanic came up to the same window and bent to talk to Mom.

"Fill 'er up, ma'am?" the mechanic asked Mom. When she looked up at him, he touched the visor of his green cap. The visor was already covered with black fingerprints.

"Yes, please," Mom told him. "Regular. And could you check the radiator please?"

The mechanic pulled open the little door on the side of Mom's Jeep and twisted the gas cap off. Mom looked at me as if surprised I was still there, and then she looked in the side view mirror at the mechanic.

"Do you have a Coke machine?" Mom asked him.

"Yes ma'am," he told her, sliding the nozzle into the Jeep. "It's right around the side there. We've got one for candy too—though most of the stuff in there's melted."

"If you have any left over, get me a Diet Coke," Mom said.

Angie crunched her way across the gravel toward the old building where Jeremy was waiting. Dylan ran after her. I strolled behind, jingling Mom's change in my palm. A root beer would taste really good right now.

"How far are we from Wellum?" I heard Mom ask the mechanic. I slowed down so I could hear his answer over the noise of the gravel underfoot.

The mechanic didn't answer right away, and that made me stop and turn around. He had been about to clean the front windshield with a squeegee, but he stopped. He set the squeegee on the hood of the Jeep and went over to Mom's open window.

"Y'all are going to Wellum?" I heard him ask, as though it surprised him for some reason.

"Yes," I heard Mom say. "I'm dropping off the kids there for a week."

"Ma'am are you sure that's a good idea?" he asked. "Have you heard what's going on over there?" He suddenly looked at me over the top of the Jeep, like he just noticed I'd been listening. I felt like I'd been caught snooping, but I just stood there.

The mechanic pulled off his cap and leaned down closer to Mom. They were talking softly now, and I couldn't make out what they were saying. I turned around and crunched across the gravel to the Coke machine, wondering what might be going on at Wellum.

I got a root beer and left the others fighting over the rest of Mom's change. It felt good to be out of the car and walking around, even though it was hot. I wandered around the front of the gas station and stood in the shade drinking my root beer. The hood on the Jeep was open now. The mechanic was checking the water level in the radiator.

I wandered to the open door of the garage. Inside was a jumble of tools and spare parts and rolling tool chests, all of them black with grease. A radio was playing country-western music somewhere in the back. There was the sound of something dripping.

I wasn't really snooping—I was just looking around, thankful to be out of the car for a few minutes. There were posters of classic cars on the wall, and an old Pepsi Cola clock that was frozen at 11:06. Scraps of metal and rusty engine parts were strewn everywhere.

Behind one of the rolling tool chests I could make out a large, black shape. It seemed soft—like someone had tossed a fur coat or a sweater on the ground. I couldn't quite make out what it was. I took another sip of root beer and tilted my head to look at it again.

Suddenly the shape moved. It barked and lunged at me from out of the shadows.

I yelled and flung my can of root beer in the air. I tore across the gravel lot toward the Jeep. Feet scrambled over the gravel behind me. Angry growls filled the air. I ran faster than I've ever run before, my heart pounding, every fiber of my body straining to propel me toward the open Jeep door.

Everyone else stood at the pumps frozen, watching me run toward them. I heard a loud sound behind me, like someone had dropped a heavy bag of loose change. The dog yelped. He'd come to the end of his chain, and it had snapped taut and flipped him over on his back on the gravel.

I looked back to see a huge black dog, thrashing around on his back, trying to get back to his feet. I stopped running and gasped for air. I bent and put my hands on my knees, trying to catch my breath.

"That's just Bruno," the man from the gas station said. "I keep him here for protection, but he really wouldn't hurt a fly."

Wouldn't hurt a fly? He'd lunged at me like a hungry lion on one of those PBS nature shows my dad likes to watch. I tried to smile and look unconcerned, but I was still gasping for air. All of us watched as the huge dog barked angrily at us a couple of times and then limped back across the gravel to plop down in the shade again.

My root beer can lay on its side by the open garage door, still leaking onto the gravel. Normally I would have picked it up and disposed of it properly, but there was no way I was going back in Bruno's range again, so I just left it where it lay. I leaned against the Jeep and took a deep breath, trying to get my heartbeat to slow down.

Chapter 2

When we pulled away from the gas station, I begged Mom to crank up the air conditioning. I was sweating bullets from the heat and from my fifty-yard dash with Bruno, the killer dog. My heart was beginning to find its normal pace again. I rubbed my damp palms on my shorts and tried to sit back and relax. In the front seat, Jeremy twisted the radio's knob, looking for a rock station. "Why can't I find anything but country music?" he complained.

"Look out the window, Einstein," I told him. "Where do you think you are?"

He switched off the radio and glared at me over his shoulder. "How would you like to *fly* out the window, you little twerp?" he asked me.

I was about to hit him with one of my snappy comebacks, but I was distracted by a tugging at my sleeve. I looked down at Dylan.

"Where's my pictures?" Dylan asked.

"What pictures?" I asked him, trying to remove his hand and get back to arguing with Jeremy.

"The pictures I drawed."

"The pictures you *drew*," I corrected, and I pulled his drawing pad from where I'd tucked it between my seat and the car door when we stopped at the gas station. "It's right here, but you *shouldn't* be drawing in the car. You're going to make yourself carsick."

Dylan grabbed the book and tugged. He started making a noise like a dentist drill. There was no point in arguing with him—Mom always sided with Dylan—so I gave him his crayons.

I looked up at Jeremy and realized that I'd already forgotten the insult I was going to say to him. I sighed. It's hard being the middle kid, especially with two brothers.

Dylan flipped through all the pictures he'd drawn on the trip so far, looking for a blank page. There were lots of boxy houses, with smoke that coiled out of their chimneys like springs. There were trees that looked more like green lollipops. Then Dylan flipped past the last picture he'd drawn.

"Wait a minute," I told him. "Go back a page."

Dylan flipped back to the last picture he'd drawn—the one he said was a gas station. I looked at it closely as we glided over those country roads.

"What did you say this one was?" I asked him.

"That's the gas station we just went to," Dylan said and started to flip the page again. I pressed the page down with my palm so he couldn't turn it. He squealed like a dentist drill again.

"This thing here," I said, pointing at the black scribble in the middle of his picture. "What did you say that was?"

"Mom—"

"Shhh," I told him. "Relax. I just want to ask you a question, and then you can turn the page."

Dylan relaxed and stopped trying to turn the page.

"This black thing you drew in front of the gas station," I asked him. "What did you say it was?"

"That's the dog that chased you."

I stared at him a minute in shock. He grinned at me and then started barking and growling. He leaned over and snapped his teeth at me, like he was going to bite me on the arm.

"Back off, you little weirdo," I told him and pushed him away.

I looked over at Angie. She'd been listening. She was looking at Dylan now with her brow furrowed.

"How did you know the dog was going to be there?" she asked.

Dylan shrugged his shoulders. "I don't know," he admitted. He flipped the page over to a new blank sheet.

"That was bizarre," Angie said to me as Dylan pried open the lid to his tin crayon box. "Has Dylan ever been to that gas station before?"

I shook my head. "Not that I know of," I told her. "Mom says we haven't been out this way since before Dylan was born."

Angie stared at Dylan with a puzzled look on her face. I didn't know what to think either. Dylan was a smart little kid—sometimes I think he's a lot smarter than I am—but even *he* couldn't tell what was going to happen before it happened. This was a pretty weird coincidence.

Dylan chose a light green crayon and wedged the tin box on the car seat between us. He was about to start drawing a new picture when Angie grabbed his hand.

"No," she told him. "I've got an idea. Why don't you draw another picture of something we're going to see down the road?"

Dylan looked at her and then turned his head to look at me—as if to ask if he should do what Angie told him. I nodded.

Dylan immediately put the green crayon back in the box beside him and rummaged around until he found the color he wanted: red-orange. Dylan propped the tablet of paper on his knees and smoothed out the top sheet.

He drew a red, squarish-looking shape, except the top was pointed, like the roof of a house. Angie and I both watched as he colored it in with the red-orange crayon. Then he found his black crayon and colored in a big square in the front.

He handed the picture to Angie. She looked at it and turned it sideways and looked at it again. She shrugged and passed it over to me.

I studied the picture. I had no idea *what* it was.

"What *is* this?" I asked Dylan. "Is this a television or something?"

"No," Dylan said, shaking his head. "I don't know what it's called."

I handed him the tablet and mussed up his hair. "It's a good picture, though," I told him. "Whatever it is."

I looked across at Angie, but she was looking past Mom out the front window. Her mouth was hanging open. I leaned in front of Dylan so I could see past Jeremy out the front window. Way down the road, on my side of the car, was a huge red barn.

Angie took the pad of paper from Dylan and looked at it and then looked at the approaching barn. The barn doors were open and it was dark inside. From a distance it looked like a big, black rectangle on the front of the barn. She handed me Dylan's picture—it *did* look a lot like the barn. I felt a chill go through me. Dylan stretched his neck to see out the side window.

As we whisked by the barn, Dylan laughed and pointed. "See," he said. "*There* it is. What's it called?"

"A barn," I told him, my mouth feeling suddenly dry. "It's called a barn."

Dylan pulled his tablet of paper out of my hands. I was too shocked to hold on to it. He propped it on his knees again and flipped to a new page.

I looked at him a few seconds. I've known him all his life, but suddenly he seemed mysterious, and—well—kind of spooky. He was giving me the heebie jeebies.

"How did you *do* that?" I asked him. "How did you know about the barn?"

Dylan just shrugged and looked at the blank sheet of paper in front of him. I looked over at Angie.

"Was that *really* a barn you drew?" Angie asked him. "I mean were you thinking of the barn when you drew the picture?"

Dylan suddenly started acting shy—the way he sometimes does when he finds himself at the center of attention. He wouldn't say anything. He just looked down at the blank paper in front of him, his chin nearly touching his chest.

I didn't know what to think. "We've got some weird stuff going on back here," I told Jeremy. He was leaning back on the headrest with his eyes closed. He mumbled something without opening his eyes.

"Dilly's got ESP or something," I said a little louder. "He keeps drawing pictures of things that haven't happened yet."

"What are you talking about?" Mom asked, laughing.

"Has Dylan ever been on this road before?" I asked her.

"No," she said. "We haven't been this way for about ten years."

"Well he keeps drawing things we're going to pass on the road before we get to them," I said. It sounded weird to say something like that out loud, especially to my mom.

"Like what?" Jeremy asked, looking back over his shoulder at me. "What did he draw?"

"Well, he just drew a picture of a barn—and then we passed that big barn back there."

Mom laughed again. Jeremy turned and peered at me over the back of his seat.

"Look out the window, Einstein," he said, using my own words against me. "Where do you think you are?" Mom laughed again.

I slouched down in my seat. Jeremy was right, of course. Even Dylan—who wasn't even in kindergarten yet—knew there were barns out in the country. He knew we'd be passing one before long; we'd passed dozens of them already. I felt like an idiot.

"It was just kind of *weird*, OK?" I said.

"There's no logical explanation I can think of," Jeremy teased. "We'd better pull over right now and call those two FBI agents on TV."

Mom laughed again. I felt even more stupid—Jeremy was good at making me feel dumb. I guess all big brothers are. "Very funny," I told him. "You should be on television yourself."

"Don't think the Comedy Channel hasn't made me some offers," he said.

"Nah," I said. "You belong on C-SPAZ." This time Mom laughed at *my* joke. I smiled to myself and looked out the window.

Deep down I knew Dylan's pictures were just dumb coincidences, but I couldn't get them out of my mind. The barn picture was easy to explain, but what about the black dog at the gas station? How could Dylan have guessed that one?

I leaned over and whispered in Dylan's ear.

"Listen, buddy," I told him. "Just draw me *one* more picture of something that's going to happen. OK?"

Dylan looked at me gravely a moment. "OK," he said.

I leaned close to him again. "But don't tell anyone else," I whispered. "Just show it to me."

Dylan rummaged through his crayon box and pulled out a silver crayon. He drew a big triangle on his pad of paper and began to color it in with the silver crayon.

Chapter 3

W ell, here we are," Mom said.

I looked up. At first I didn't know what she was talking about; it looked like we were still in the middle of nowhere. There were bushes on both sides of the road as far as I could see, but Mom slowed the car down.

Suddenly a gap appeared in the bushes, and next to the gap was a dented mail box with the number 51 on it. It had a few holes in it, like someone had been using it for target practice.

We turned on to a narrow dirt driveway that was really just two ruts worn in the grassy ground. The drive curved around a clump of bushes and then went straight toward a grove of trees in the distance. Mom drove very slowly along the bumpy road. All I could see ahead of us was trees.

"There is a *house* here, isn't there?" I asked. "Uncle Allen doesn't live in some kind of hollowed-out tree trunk does he?"

"Uncle Allen has a very nice house," Mom said. "And it's at least *twice* the size of our house."

The rutted road bounced the Jeep around. Dylan was still trying to draw with his crayons, even though he was getting tossed from side to side by the movement of the car.

When I looked out the window again, I glimpsed the white pointed roof of a house rising among the grove of trees we were approaching. As we drove closer to the trees, the house disappeared again. The road wound among the tree trunks, deep in shadow, and then suddenly we were out in the bright sunlight, pulling up in front of a huge house.

I couldn't see the house very well, because I was sitting on the opposite side of the car, but Angie twisted her neck to look up at it through her window. Her mouth hung open in amazement. "It's like the Munster's house," she said.

"It's nothing like the Munster's house," my mom said. "It's a very nice Victorian house. A lot of these old places have them. They were the style when people first started farming here."

Jeremy had dozed off in the front seat, so I unbuckled my seat belt, leaned forward and rapped the top of his head with my knuckle. "Yo," I said. "Anybody home? Wake up. We're here."

I felt excited all of a sudden, and I wanted to see where we'd be staying for the next week. I opened the car door, stepped out into the heat, and gazed up at the house.

It was truly amazing. It had a broad front porch that seemed to encircle the entire house. It had scrolled balconies, a round tower at one corner and a railed walkway around the top of the roof—I think they call it a widow's walk. None of the windows lined up, but it seemed like it was *at least* three stories tall. This huge, fancy house seemed out of place at the end of a winding dirt road like this, in the middle of nowhere.

I tried to picture our house back in the city. Mom was wrong—Uncle Allen's place must have been at least *four or five times* as big as our house.

"Uncle Allen lives in there *alone?*" I asked.

Mom nodded. "Back in the old days, the whole family lived here—the parents, children, even the grandkids. Sometimes there were four generations living under this one roof."

"And Uncle Allen's the only one left?" Angie asked.

25

"Yes," Mom said. "Everyone else moved to the city. He's the only farmer left in the family. He lives here all by himself."

Jeremy opened his car door and stood up to look over the car at the house. He whistled. "Man!" he said, running his fingers back through his hair. "That house would be worth a million dollars if it were in the city."

"Yes," Mom agreed. "But they're a dime a dozen out here. Not many people want to live so far from town."

Mom led us up the front steps and across the broad porch to the door. The house was huge, but the door was narrow; and it had a small, triangular stained-glass window near the top.

Mom knocked.

We all stood waiting. Dylan hopped on one foot like he had to go to the bathroom. Mom knocked again. There was no answer.

"I was afraid of this," she said. "I don't think he's home."

"Where is he?" I asked.

"He could be out in the fields working," she said. "Or he may have gone to the general store to get some supplies because he knew you kids were coming. It's just down the road a few miles."

"What are we going to do?" Angie asked.

Mom looked down at Dylan, who was hopping around, looking up at her pleadingly. "I guess we'll just go inside," Mom said. She twisted the door knob and pushed it open. She led us through the door into a broad, dark front hall, holding Dylan by the hand. "No one out here locks their doors," she explained. "It's not like in the city. It's safe out here."

At the end of the front hall, she stopped at the foot of a staircase. "Uncle Allen?" she called up the stairs. "Uncle Allen?" There was still no answer.

Mom turned and looked at Jeremy, Angie, and me. She sighed. "OK," she told us. "He's definitely not here. I'll take Dilly to the restroom. You three start unloading your stuff from the car."

I went outside and helped Jeremy pull the two bikes off the rack on the back of the Jeep. We rolled them over and laid them down on the grass next to the porch steps. Then we carried all the luggage and the sleeping bags into the house and set them in the big front hallway, next to a heavy entry table that was pushed against the wall.

An hour later, Uncle Allen still had not returned, but Mom could wait no longer.

"I've got to get back," she told us. "I've still got to drop Dylan off at your Aunt Melody's—and I've got all the packing to do tonight." She looked at Jeremy, then me, then Angie. "You three think you'll be OK here on your own for a while?"

"Huh?" I said.

"I'm sure Uncle Allen will be back before dark," Mom told me. "Can you kids wait for him on your own?"

I looked around. We were sitting in a dim, dusty, cobwebby front parlor full of old pictures and knobby furniture. It smelled stale and musty. I guess Uncle Allen didn't have a lot of time for housekeeping. I looked at Angie. She didn't look thrilled with the idea of being here alone either.

"No problem," Jeremy said, smiling. "I'll baby-sit these two till Uncle Allen gets here."

Mom looked at me. "You think you guys will be OK on your own?" she asked me. The creepy old house moaned suddenly and a breeze billowed out the lace curtains. I ran a finger around the inside of my collar and swallowed hard. "No problem," I told her.

Mom sat in the driver's seat with the car running. Jeremy and Angie had gone back inside already. "You're sure you're going to be OK?" she asked through the open window.

I looked back at the spooky old house. I could see Jeremy and Angie through the parlor window.

"You're *sure* this is the right place?" I asked her.

She laughed. "Of course it is," she told me. "And I'm sure Uncle Allen will be home any minute. You just do what he tells you, and you'll be fine."

She leaned her head out the window, and I kissed her good-bye.

"Remember," she said. "Uncle Allen has spent most of his life out here all by himself. He isn't used to having people around, and he doesn't know many children. So be quiet and obedient, and try not to get in his way."

I must have looked pretty nervous.

"Don't worry," she told me. "You'll all get along fine." She turned to Dylan. "Say good-bye to your brother," she told him.

I went around to the passenger side of the car. Dylan struggled to roll down his window.

"I'll miss you, little buddy," I told him, mussing up his hair.

"Don't you want the picture?" he asked me.

"What picture?"

"The one of what's going to happen next," he said. "You told me you wanted it."

I'd been so distracted by Uncle Allen's house, I'd completely forgotten the picture I'd asked Dylan to draw. *Crayon drawing of the future!* It all seemed silly now.

"Make it quick," Mom told Dylan, looking at the clock on the car radio. "We should have left half an hour ago."

Dylan bit his lower lip while he concentrated on tearing his latest picture from the pad of paper. Then he passed the picture to me through the window. I stared at it and tried to look enthusiastic. I had no idea what it was supposed to be. It was a large silver triangle with a circle in the middle. Inside the circle he had drawn what looked like three faces.

"Is this all of us driving in the car?" I guessed. "How come there's only three faces?"

Dylan reached a chubby arm out the window and pointed to the faces. "This is you, and Angie, and Jeremy," he said.

"Let's go, you two," Mom told us. "We've got to leave right now."

"What's this we're in?" I asked Dylan turning the picture toward him.

"You're in the flying saucer," he said as the car started to pull away. "The one that's going to take you away."

"Bye," Mom called, waving back at me.

"Bye, Ryan," Dylan yelled, as the car disappeared among the trees.

Flying saucer? The one that's going to take us away? I looked down at the picture I was holding and swallowed hard.

Chapter 4

I'm not one of those guys who sits around all day reading comic books about swamp creatures or watching videos about alien autopsies. I don't spend a lot of time on the Internet looking up Bigfoot or the Loch Ness Monster. I don't really believe in any of that stuff.

But when Dylan showed me the picture of us being abducted by a UFO—after the pictures of the black dog and the red barn—I've got to admit it spooked me just a little. If I'd been at home, I would have just laughed it off—but you've got to remember that we'd just been dropped off at a big, spooky house full of cobwebs and dust, out in the middle of nowhere, to stay with a man none of us knew.

I stood looking at the grove of trees where Mom's Cherokee had disappeared, and I have to admit that I had the impulse to sprint after the Jeep and beg Mom to take me with them—but of course I didn't.

I turned around and looked at the big, old Victorian house. The afternoon light cast long shadows across the building's face and made all the windows glow softly. I took a deep breath, puffed up my cheeks, and then exhaled noisily. It was *not* a sigh of relief.

Why couldn't Dylan have drawn a picture of people riding horses or flying kites—the way little kids are supposed to? But *no—my* little brother had to draw a picture of an alien abduction. I folded the picture and put it in the back pocket of my jeans. I climbed the creaky front steps and walked across the wooden porch to the front door.

I twisted the doorknob. No one locked their doors in the country, Mom had told us. It was safe out here. They didn't have to worry about burglars.

But what about *little green men?*

I wanted to wait right where we were—in the parlor, with all our suitcases and sleeping bags piled in the front hall. I wanted to stay right there, with all the curtains open and all the lights turned on. After all, none of us really *knew* Uncle Allen, and he could be getting back at any minute. But Jeremy had other ideas.

"What if he comes home?" I asked. "He might not like finding us exploring his house."

"Are you kidding?" Jeremy said. "It's going to be pitch black in an hour. We should get ourselves situated. We should start to unpack."

"But we don't know where he wants us to stay," I pointed out. "He's probably got some rooms set up for us."

"Will you look at this place?" Jeremy waved his hand at the cluttered, dusty front room we were sitting in. "Does it look like he's spent a lot of time preparing for our visit? He's a busy man. He works this whole farm by himself. He probably hasn't even *been* in most of the rooms in this place for years."

I knew he was right. Uncle Allen probably worked from dawn to dark every day. He probably lived on the ground floor and ignored the rest of the house—it was much too big for one person.

Still, the thought of the three of us going upstairs and looking around without Mom there kind of gave me the creeps.

"I'll bet we can each pick our own room," Jeremy said. "Maybe even our own *floors*. Let's go see what we can find."

Angie and I reluctantly followed Jeremy to the foot of the stairs. Jeremy climbed up a couple of steps and then stood there, holding the banister with one hand, looking up into the shadows. The wooden steps were rutted from all the feet that had climbed them in the past hundred years.

I don't know a lot about old Victorian houses, but I'll tell you one thing: they're dark inside. The windows are small, and all the rooms seem kind of shadowy, even with the afternoon sun shining through the lace curtains. Over the staircase hung a light, but there was no bulb in the socket.

Jeremy just stood there a moment longer. I could tell he was spooked, though he tried to hide it. When he started climbing the steps, I stayed a step or two behind him. Angie came up last.

On the second floor, Jeremy felt around on the wall for a light switch. When he flipped it on, we saw a long narrow hallway that ran past a few doorways, up three steps and past some more doors. At the end of the hall was a narrow spiral staircase that twisted up into the shadows. That's where Jeremy took us.

"Where are we going?" I asked, as Jeremy started up the second staircase. "There are plenty of rooms on this floor. Why don't we just stay here?"

"I want the room in the tower," he told us, disappearing around the bend in the staircase. I didn't want to follow him to the third floor, but I didn't want to look like a "feeb" in front of Angie either. I stood there, listening to Jeremy's footsteps creak across the ceiling above our heads. I admit it; I was scared.

I looked at Angie, I could tell she was scared, too. She closed her eyes, and I wondered if she was saying a prayer.

"Ready?" Angie asked. She was still nervous, but she didn't seem as *frightened* any more—if that makes any sense.

I took a deep breath and started climbing the dark spiraling stairs.

The third floor hallway was much darker and even hotter than the second. It was lit only by the sunlight shining through one of the open doorways near the end. I felt on the wall for a light switch. When I found it I flipped it up and down. Nothing happened.

"No light bulbs," Jeremy called to me from down the hall. "I already tried." I could see his shadowy shape open a doorway at the very end of the hall and let more light in.

More light seemed like a good idea to me, so as I continued down the hall I pushed open each closed door. Every brass doorknob was powdered with dust.

"I'll bet no one's been up here in ten years," Angie said close behind me.

The rooms had no furniture—just bare wooden floors and peeling wallpaper. In some of the rooms I saw the footprints of mice on the dusty floorboards or lighter ovals and rectangles on the wall where pictures had once hung.

When Angie and I caught up with Jeremy, he was standing in the last room—the round room in the tower. He pulled open the heavy curtains on the room's one window. When the light streamed in we could see dust swirling in the beams of light.

"Honey, I'm home," Jeremy shouted, the way Dad sometimes does when he opens the front door. He seemed very pleased with his new room.

I looked around at the stained wallpaper and the worn wooden floor. I felt a drip of sweat creep down my side under my shirt—it was awfully hot up here.

"There's no furniture in here," I pointed out. "Where are you going to sleep?"

"My sleeping bag," he told me. "I'll just drag a mattress up here from one of the rooms downstairs and throw it on the floor. And I can borrow a couple of light bulbs from downstairs too."

He unlatched the window, pulled it open and stood back. "Feel that cool afternoon breeze," he said as if he were a real estate agent trying to make a big sale.

Angie and I found rooms on the second floor, where there was furniture and electric lights and where it wasn't quite as hot. I checked every room and opened every window that wasn't painted shut to try to get some ventilation.

Uncle Allen's room must have been on the ground floor, because all of the beds on the second floor were stripped bare. Angie chose a room in the front of the house with a big bay window that looked out on the grove of trees and the front drive. Even though the sun had almost disappeared behind the trees, it was the brightest room in the house.

I picked a small room under the spiral staircase. It wasn't much to look at—just a brass bed with a lumpy mattress, a small desk, and a bookcase full of old books. What I liked about it was the small, wood-framed glass door that led out to a balcony on the side of the house. I've always thought it would be cool to have a balcony. I propped the glass door open with my backpack full of clothes, so the afternoon breeze could air out the room, which smelled of musty books.

I stepped out onto the balcony and looked out at the fields that spread in all directions. Uncle Allen had a small barn next to the house and below my balcony was a small pen with a goat inside. The goat just stood there working its jaw, though I couldn't see anything around it could possibly be eating.

"Let's go," Jeremy called from my doorway. "Let's unpack."

All of us dragged our things up to our chosen rooms, and Jeremy took a couple of light bulbs from the empty rooms on our floor so he could have some light upstairs. Before the sky grew dark, we rolled the bikes up on the porch and leaned them against the railing.

Back up in my room, I finished unpacking. When I was done, I went over to the bookcase to see what kinds of books Uncle Allen had—I hadn't brought along any books to read.

The old books were mostly about farming, but there was also a huge family Bible. I pulled it off the shelf and hefted it over to the bed. It was dusty and the binding felt like it was coming loose. In the front of the Bible it had a list of names under the word BIRTHS.

I ran my finger down the names and found Uncle Allen, and then Mom and Angie's mom as well. Whoever had been filling in the names stopped a long time ago—none of us kids were listed, though there were plenty of empty spaces.

I flipped the Bible open to somewhere near the middle and my eyes stopped on Psalm 139:

> *Wither shall I go from thy spirit?*
> *Or wither shall I flee from thy presence?*
> *If I ascend up into heaven, thou art*
> *   there:*
> *if I make my bed in hell, behold, thou art*
> *   there.*
> *If I take the wings of the morning,*
> *and dwell in the uttermost parts of the*
> *   sea;*
> *Even there shall thy hand lead me,*
> *and thy right hand shall hold me.*
> *If I say, Surely the darkness shall cover*
> *   me;*
> *even the night shall be light about me.*
> *Yea, the darkness hideth not from thee;*
> *but the night shineth as the day;*
> *the darkness and the light are both alike*
> *   to thee.*

I wasn't sure what all the words meant, but I thought about Angie and the prayer she said when we were about to go up the dark staircase. *It would be nice to feel that way*, I thought.

Chapter 5

After nine o'clock, we gave up waiting for Uncle Allen. All of us were hungry, especially Jeremy. The three of us went in the kitchen to see what we could find to eat. Because it was dark, we all stayed close together.

There was an oval table with four chairs in the middle of the kitchen. To the left was a door that led outside. The top half of the door was a pane of glass. Outside, the night was jet black. Jeremy opened the small refrigerator and bent to look inside. I peered over his shoulder. There was hardly anything inside—just a big glass pitcher of milk, four eggs, a brown paper bag full of string beans, and a pint of lemon yogurt.

"Uncle Allen must do a lot of entertaining," Jeremy said.

"He's a regular Martha Stewart," Angie said. "There must be some food here somewhere."

Angie looked through the lower cupboards, and I dragged a chair from the table and stood on it so I could look in the higher ones. Most of the cupboards were empty—empty of food, anyway. There was plenty of dust and cockroaches and spider webs.

"Maybe he just grazes out back with the goat," I suggested.

I pulled the chair back over to the table. My hands felt dusty, so I washed them at the sink and dried them on a dishtowel.

"Eureka!" Angie said as she opened what I thought was a broom closet. It turned out to be a pantry. Jeremy and I crowded around to see what was inside.

The pantry had a few cans on one shelf, and a box of plain oatmeal on another.

"On tonight's menu," Angie announced, turning the cans so she could read the labels, "we have a small can of coffee, two cans of rhubarb, a can of pear halves in their own juice, and a large can of baked beans."

"Perfect," Jeremy joked. "Those are exactly the ingredients I need for my famous *pears a la barfé*."

"*Barfé* is right," Angie said.

"Let's just eat the beans," I suggested. "Maybe that'll hold us over until Uncle Allen gets home and shows us where he keeps the *real* food."

Ten minutes later the three of us sat around the table, steaming bowls of beans in front of us. Jeremy dug right in, but Angie bowed her head.

I looked at Jeremy. His mouth was crammed full of beans. He stopped chewing suddenly.

"Why don't you say grace for all of us?" I said to Angie. She opened her eyes and smiled.

"Sure," she said. "I'd be happy to."

We all bowed our heads and closed our eyes. I could hear Jeremy breathing loudly through his nose, his mouth still crammed full of beans.

"Thank you for this food," Angie prayed. "And thank you for bringing us safely here. Watch over our parents this week as they travel far away. And please keep us safe from harm. Amen."

I opened my eyes. Jeremy started chewing again.

As we ate, I kept listening for Uncle Allen to come through the front door, but he never did.

After dinner we went to our rooms to unpack our stuff.

I stepped out onto the balcony to look up at the sky, which was crowded with stars. Just then, I saw the lights of a pickup truck bouncing along the grassy road toward the house.

"He's here!" I shouted, dashing through my room and out into the second floor hallway. "Uncle Allen is finally here!"

I ran down the hallway to Angie's room, where Jeremy was helping her move some furniture. "Let's go, you guys," I shouted. "He's here."

The three of us ran downstairs and into the front hallway. I pulled open the front door and we burst out onto the porch. There was a light on in the hallway, so I pulled the door shut behind us, to prevent any bugs from following the light inside.

The truck's headlights lit up the lower branches of the dark trees, coming steadily toward us, until the pickup pulled into the clearing in front of the house. The headlights swept across the front porch. I squinted and turned my head. The truck disappeared around the side of the house.

"Is that him?" Angie asked.

"Who *else* could find this place?" Jeremy said. "We're off the map here. It's got to be him. He's probably coming in the kitchen door."

We turned to go back inside, but when I tried to open the front door it was locked. I shook the door.

"Smooth," Jeremy told me. "You better *hope* that's Uncle Allen who just pulled up and not some crazed dude with an ax."

The three of us crossed the creaking porch in the darkness, sticking close together, and felt our way down the front steps.

In the city, you forget how dark it can get. But out in the country––where there are no street lights or cars passing by—the night is so black, it feels like you could *lean* against the darkness. It was more than a little spooky. We huddled together and found our way around the side of the house.

In the light that shone through the glass in the kitchen door, I could see the faint outline of a pickup truck parked in the tall grass. When we got closer we could hear the hot engine ticking.

We crept past the truck and made our way toward the light from the window in the kitchen door. I climbed the kitchen steps with the other two close behind me, anxious to get safely inside. I was reaching to knock on the door when I froze in my tracks.

There in the bright kitchen stood the creepiest looking man I had ever seen. He was tall and very skinny, and his skin had a grayish tint to it. He was completely bald and his head looked much too large and broad for his body. At the end of his thin arms were long hands with nervous, twig-like fingers.

"What's the matter?" Angie whispered from the step below me.

She stood on her tiptoes and peered over my shoulder. When she looked through the window she let out a little gasp.

"Who *is* that?" she said.

"What *planet* does he come from?" Jeremy said. "That's what *I'd* like to know."

The man inside the kitchen—if he *was* a man—slowly opened a cupboard door, got down a mug and plate and set them on the counter. He moved slowly and deliberately, like he wasn't used to his arms and legs. He went over to the refrigerator with the mug, opened the door and reached inside.

I expected him to take out the pitcher of milk, but instead he grabbed the four eggs with the long, slender fingers of one hand. He closed the refrigerator door and went to the sink.

One at a time he cracked the eggs and dumped them into the mug.

"There go the rhubarb and coffee omelets I was going to make us all for breakfast," Jeremy whispered.

"That's *disgusting*," Angie told him.

Just then, the man in the kitchen noticed the empty tin can we'd left sitting on the kitchen counter next to the sink after we cooked the baked beans. He scowled at it for a moment.

Slowly he tilted his head to look at the ceiling, his mouth open a little. His eyes rolled slowly around in his massive head, as though he were listening for signs of life in the empty house. Hearing nothing, and still scowling, he raised the mug of raw eggs to his lips and drank them down.

"Now *that's* disgusting," Jeremy said.

The man went back to the refrigerator and got out the bag of string beans and the quart of lemon yogurt. He pulled out a chair and sat down at the table. He grabbed a string bean from the brown paper bag. Like he was dipping a french fry in ketchup, the man dunked the string bean into the lemon yogurt. He held it in front of his face looking at it, and then bit into it.

"Oh, *man*," Jeremy whispered. "Even *I* got grossed out by that one."

"What should we do?" I asked.

"Knock on the door," Jeremy said. "I'm getting bit by mosquitoes."

"How do we know that's Uncle Allen?" Angie asked.

"Who *else* would it be?" Jeremy said.

One by one, the man at the table dipped the green beans in the yogurt and ate them. Like a bunch of dummies, we stood and watched him through the kitchen door.

"Knock on the door," Jeremy told me. "It's crazy to just stand out here."

"*You* knock on the door," I told him.

Jeremy didn't move. He would never admit it, but I could tell he was as scared of Uncle Allen as I was.

"We can't stand here all night," Jeremy pointed out. I looked at his face, which seemed pale in the faint light coming through the glass. "One of us should do something."

"Go on in and introduce yourself," Angie whispered, calling his bluff. "Ryan and I will wait out here for a formal invita—"

Angie stopped in midsentence. Her eyes were wide with fright. She stared through the window and her lips moved as if she was trying to speak.

I glanced through the window and my stomach clenched suddenly. The man at the table was glaring directly at us. He appeared to be shocked and angry. He placed his palms on the tabletop and slowly rose to his feet.

I took a step back, forgetting that I was standing on the kitchen steps. I began to fall and grabbed at Jeremy's arm, pulling him down with me. He knocked over Angie, and the three of us tumbled backward into the tall grass, landing in a heap. Poor Angie ended up on the bottom.

"Get off me, you big oafs," she grunted.

Suddenly the kitchen door swung open and we were flooded with light.

"Who are you?" an angry, droning voice demanded. With the light from the kitchen behind him, all we could see was a strange silhouette towering over us—with a large head, long arms, and bony fingers. He *did* look like something from another planet.

I was struck speechless. My lips moved, but no sound came out.

"Who are you?" the voice boomed again.

"He's Ryan," Jeremy said, pointing at me.

"Thanks a lot," I managed to mumble.

I felt Angie squirming beneath me. She slapped at my back.

"Get off me," she said. "You're hurting my leg." She pushed me so hard I rolled backwards into the weeds. Angie sat up. "Are you Uncle Allen?" she asked as she brushed a blade of loose grass from her face.

The man scowled down at us curiously for a moment without saying a word, as though he didn't understand the question. "Yes," he said at last. "I am Uncle Allen."

Chapter 6

No one was much in the mood for conversation, especially Uncle Allen. He didn't seem pleased to have us visiting, so we excused ourselves from the kitchen as soon as we could and escaped upstairs to Jeremy's room.

Uncle Allen gave me the willies, and being way up on the third floor felt better because we were as far away from him as we could be without leaving the house. Believe it or not, it felt less spooky up there, even though there were only two working lights on the whole floor—one in Jeremy's round room and one outside in the hallway.

Angie sat on the mattress with her back against the wall reading her Bible, while Jeremy and I sat on the floor playing boxes—that game where you try to make as many squares as you can by connecting dots on a piece of paper.

"I don't know what you two are talking about," Jeremy said, passing me the pencil. "I think Uncle Allen is absolutely charming."

"Mom told me he might be a bit unusual because he wasn't used to being around other people," I said. "But this is ridiculous."

"I'm still grossed out from those raw eggs," Angie said without looking up from her reading.

I waited until Jeremy wasn't looking and connected a couple of dots. I handed him the pencil. "Your turn."

"Where did you go?" Jeremy asked, looking down at the paper.

"I don't have to tell you," I said. "You snooze, you lose."

Jeremy angled the paper under the bare light bulb and studied it, trying to find where I'd left my mark.

"Maybe he has some kind of vitamin deficiency," Angie said more to herself than to anyone else.

"Aha!" Jeremy said, grinning down at the paper. "You thought I wouldn't notice." He quickly completed a long row of boxes and began writing his initials in each one.

"Or maybe he's on some kind of weird new diet," Angie said.

"If he lost any more weight, he'd vanish," Jeremy pointed out.

"Whatever his problem is, he gives me the creeps," I said. "He seems mean. I don't know if I can take a week of this."

"Aw, don't be so lame," Jeremy said. "You don't need to be afraid of him. He's just a harmless old hermit with a head the size of a watermelon. We've got the run of this place. It'll be like a week with no parents. We can have all kinds of fun." Jeremy passed me the pencil and paper. "You're up," he said.

I was about to complete a box, when the door suddenly flew open. Angie screamed. Her Bible flew up in the air and thumped against the wall behind her. My pencil skidded across the paper. Jeremy, who was sitting with his back to the door, scrambled around to see what was happening.

Uncle Allen stood in the doorway scowling down at us. He looked behind us and shook his large head gravely. He crossed the room to the open window. As he passed by, Jeremy and I scooted backward out of his way and Angie pressed herself against the wall.

Uncle Allen pulled the window closed and latched it. Then he looked out the window at the night sky. Jeremy looked at me. His eyes were wide. He'd never admit it, but I could tell he was scared.

"Sir, it's kind of hot in here," I said meekly, my mouth dry. "We were really enjoying the breeze."

Uncle Allen didn't move. For what seemed like eternity, he just stood there, looking out the window. "If you know what's good for you, you'll keep this window shut tight at night," he said gruffly. "Make sure *all* the windows and doors are shut. And whatever you do, don't go outside after dark."

He peered through the window for another minute and then turned and disappeared out the door. We sat silently and listened to his footsteps recede down the stairs and then clump along the hallway beneath us.

"Tell me again why I shouldn't be afraid of the 'old hermit,'" I said to my brother.

Jeremy didn't say a word. Finally he blew out the breath he'd been holding and stretched his hands out in front of him. They were shaking.

"Do you think he heard us talking about him?" Angie asked, looking at the open door.

"I don't know," I said.

Jeremy stood and walked to the window. He squinted out at the sky. "What do you suppose he was looking at?" he mumbled.

"I thought your mom said no one locks their doors or windows out here," Angie said.

I shrugged. Angie stood up and joined Jeremy at the window, looking up at the sky. I struggled to my feet. On shaky legs I walked over and shut off the light.

"Aaah!" Angie and Jeremy yelled in unison.

"Oops, sorry guys, "I said, "but it's a whole lot easier to see outside with the lights off."

"D-don't do that again," Jeremy said.

I inched my way across the pitch black room to the window, and peered out over Jeremy's shoulder.

"What do you suppose is out there?" Jeremy said.

"And why can't we go outside after dark?" Angie added.

My nerves were jangled. I kept thinking about Dylan's picture and the man at the gas station. What was happening here? Who was this strange-looking man we were trapped with in this house? And what was going on outside? I shivered, even though the room was stuffy with the window latched and there was no breeze.

"Did you guys see that last picture Dylan drew?" I asked.

"No," Angie told me, still looking out the window. "What did he draw?"

I looked up at the twinkling stars.

"Nothing," I told her. "It really wasn't anything important."

Chapter 7

I don't know what woke me up. All I know is that I looked around in the dark, strange room and groaned when I remembered where I was. I was lying on top of the covers because it was so hot without any windows open. I'd been dreaming that I was at home with Mom, Dad, and Dylan and we were getting ready to eat dinner. But now, awake, everything that had happened that day came flooding back. I was not a happy camper.

I lay on my back and put my hands behind my head. I knew it would be hard to get back to sleep because of the heat. I was tempted to get up and pry open the glass door to the balcony for some fresh air—but I couldn't bring myself to do it. Uncle Allen scared me. I *had* to do what he said—even though he'd never know if I opened a window or not.

I tried to relax. It would only be a week, I reminded myself. Just six more nights of sleeping in this bed and I'd be back home where I belonged.

I stared up at the ceiling, trying to give myself a pep talk. You'll have fun, I told myself. You'll explore the farm. You'll have a great time with Jeremy and Angie—and once you get to know Uncle Allen, he won't seem so weird. Everything will look better in the light of day.

Just then, I noticed some faint lights shimmer across the ceiling—like the ones that crossed my bedroom ceiling back home when a car passed, late at night, on the street outside my window. But out here we were about a half mile from the nearest highway.

It occurred to me that maybe someone was coming up the grassy driveway to the house. For a few seconds I entertained the notion that maybe Mom had come back to get us and was now pulling up outside the house—but I knew that wasn't very likely. And my room was on the side of the house, not the front. The lights couldn't be from the drive-way.

I stared at the ceiling for a few minutes, but the lights were gone. I looked around the room. Maybe it was a reflection, but there was hardly anything in the room, and what was there was coated with dust—none of it could make a reflection.

I had just about decided it was all in my imagination, when I looked back at the ceiling and saw the light skim across it again. I was spooked, and I wished I hadn't picked a room so far away from Jeremy and Angie.

I got out of bed and tiptoed to the glass door. The glass was streaked with dust, but I could still see through it. I cupped my hands against the glass and looked out. It was nothing like the night sky at home, where I can sometimes make out the Big Dipper and not a whole lot more.

The land and all the trees near the house were black, and above them stretched a dome of shimmering bright lights. I could clearly see the faint white streak of the Milky Way stretched like a ragged ribbon over the dark farmland. The sky was sparkling and lonely, like when you stand on a dark hill and look down on the city at night. It was beautiful in an eerie kind of way. I felt a lump begin to grow in my throat again, when I thought about how far away my family was.

As I stood staring into the darkness, something strange and impossible happened. Three bright lights suddenly streaked upward out of the fields on the other side of the trees across the yard. They formed a perfect triangle, without a sound, about a hundred yards away from where I was standing.

I was so shocked, I felt like something had hit me in the chest—I stumbled backward and sat down on the bed. *What in the world was that?* I asked myself. I tried to keep it out of my mind, but all I could think of was the last picture Dylan drew for me—the one where Jeremy, Angie and I were being taken away in a triangular flying saucer. My heart began jackhammering in my chest. *No,* I told myself. *It's impossible.*

I crept back to the glass door and peeked out. The night sky was back to normal. Whatever it was that had rocketed up out of the field on the other side of Uncle Allen's trees was gone. It was probably miles away by now—at least I hoped it was.

I pulled the musty curtains closed and sat down on the bed. I huddled in the dark for a few minutes, trying to convince myself that it was just my imagination. Each creak of the old house made me jump. Each sound of a mouse scuttling across a floor somewhere set my heart racing. I wanted to believe that I'd been dreaming, but I couldn't deny that I was wide awake now—and I had no chance of getting back to sleep!

I pulled on my shorts and tiptoed to the door. I inched it open a crack and peeked down the dark hallway. I held my breath and listened, then slipped out the door and crept up the creaking spiral stairway to the third floor. Jeremy had turned off the hallway light, so I felt my way along the dusty walls in complete darkness until I was outside his room. It was the only one with the door closed.

I knocked quietly on his door, but when there was no answer I knocked again a bit more loudly. I got that creepy feeling—like someone was watching me—even though I knew I was alone. In spite of the heat, I felt a chill go through me.

I knocked again and pressed my ear to the door. I could hear Jeremy stirring. I heard a mumbling sound, which I took to be an invitation to come inside.

I pushed open Jeremy's door. In the darkness I could make out his shape curled up on a mattress on the floor. He was sleeping on top of his sleeping bag. It was even hotter up here than back in my room.

"Jeremy?" I asked. "Jeremy, are you awake?" He twitched a little, but didn't say anything.

I stepped over him and tiptoed to the window. I crouched low and peeked out. All I could see were the dark shapes of the trees and the brilliant, starry sky. Nothing was out there. I pulled the curtain shut and kneeled down on the floor beside Jeremy's mattress. I poked him with my finger.

"What? What?" he yelled, rolling over suddenly and sitting bolt upright.

"It's just me," I said, trying to calm him down. "It's Ryan. I think I saw something."

He looked around in the darkness and rubbed his neck.

"You what?" he asked groggily. I could tell he was annoyed.

"I think I *saw* something," I told him. "Down in my room. Something really weird."

He yawned. "I was *sleeping*," he told me.

"No duh," I said. "Wake up. This is important."

"What is?"

My knees hurt from kneeling on the hard floor, so I sat down on the edge of the mattress. "Remember how Uncle Allen stared out the window, and you were wondering what he was looking for?"

"Yeah?" he said. "So?"

"Don't you think its kind of weird that he insisted we keep the windows shut tight?"

"Huh?"

"Doesn't it strike you that there's something peculiar going on here?"

"What is this, Twenty Questions?" Jeremy said rubbing his eyes. "Is there a point here, or have you lost your mind?"

"Keep your voice down," I pleaded. "I'm worried that something terrible is going to happen."

"What?" he asked angrily. "*What* do you think is going to happen?"

"If I tell you, you'll think I'm crazy."

"I *already* think you're crazy," he pointed out. "And waking me up at this hour isn't helping your case."

"*OK*," I said. "OK, I'll tell you." I look a deep breath and then blurted out what was on my mind. "I think we're in danger of being abducted by aliens," I told him.

Jeremy looked over at me and grinned in the dark. He made a show of cleaning out his ears with his index fingers. "How's that?" he asked.

I felt myself blush. It sounded really stupid when I said it out loud. "I think we're going to be abducted by aliens," I said softly. "I think I just saw a UFO outside."

Jeremy was silent for a few seconds and then he started to laugh. "I think they already abducted your *brain*, Ryan."

"I'm serious. I saw something outside my window just now. There were these lights, and they rose up out of the field and disappeared into the sky. It looked like the lights on some kind of huge spaceship."

"It was probably the planet Venus," Jeremy said. "People are always mistaking it for a plane or a UFO."

"There aren't *three* planet Venuses are there?"

Jeremy sighed. "Look, there's some kind of reasonable explanation for what you saw," he said. "I don't know what it was, but it definitely *wasn't* a flying saucer. You might have been dreaming or something."

"There's more," I said. I reached in the back pocket of my shorts and pulled out the picture Dylan had given me before he left. I handed it to Jeremy in the darkness. He just sat there, like he was waiting for something.

"Could you pass me my night-vision goggles?" Jeremy asked.

I glanced around the room. "Huh?" I said.

"Turn on the light, you big dope," he told me. "How am I supposed to see this in the dark?"

"Oh," I said. "Right." I went to the doorway and found the light switch. Suddenly the room was flooded with blinding light from the bare light bulb hanging from the ceiling. I blinked and squinted till my eyes adjusted.

I looked at the window. I wondered whether anyone was watching the house from outside and had seen the light go on in Jeremy's third-floor window. The thought gave me the shivers.

Jeremy turned the picture upside down and right side up again. His hair was sticking up all over the place. "What's this supposed to be?"

"Dylan drew it," I told him.

Jeremy groaned. *"And?"*

"Remember those pictures Dylan was drawing on the way out here in the car?" I asked him. "Remember how they all came true?"

He sighed loudly. "If you say so," he said.

"Well, he gave this to me as he was leaving," I explained. "He said it was you, me, and Angie being taken away in a flying saucer."

Jeremy stared at me a few seconds. "That's it," he said. "I've had enough. I'm going back to sleep." He rolled over and covered his head with his pillow.

"Aren't you going to help me?"

"A team of psychologists working around the clock couldn't help you," Jeremy told me, his voice muffled by the pillow. "Your kid brother draws some dumb picture, and suddenly you think you're being chased by Martians."

I knew he was right. Sometimes you can get some pretty dumb ideas in your head when it's late at night—especially when you're away from home.

But I also knew I wasn't going to get any sleep down in my room.

"Jeremy," I said. "You think it would be OK if I stayed up here with you?"

Jeremy sighed and scooted over on the mattress. "Just turn off the light and try not to snore," he told me.

Chapter 8

The next morning I was almost too embarrassed to come downstairs for breakfast. When I woke up in Jeremy's room, he was already gone. His empty sleeping bag lay in a heap on the mattress next to me. I cringed when I remembered the night before and all that I'd said to Jeremy. He'd never let me forget it.

I yawned, got up off the mattress, and went to the window. Outside, the sun was already quite high in the sky. All I could see were trees and beautiful green fields stretching out in all directions. It was a glorious, sunny morning, and it made me feel like an idiot that I'd been so scared the night before.

I went down to my own room to get dressed. The view from the glass door didn't look any more sinister than the view from Jeremy's window. I opened the glass door and went out on the balcony. Uncle Allen hadn't said anything about going out during the daytime. I looked out over the trees and the fields where I'd seen the strange lights in the sky the night before. I wondered if those lights were what Uncle Allen had been looking for when he stormed into Jeremy's room to close the window. I wondered if he had something to do with them.

I went back inside and latched the door tight.

I sat on the bed and buttoned up my shirt. I could hear Jeremy and Angie moving around downstairs in the kitchen.

In a few minutes I crept down the stairs feeling sheepish. I only hoped that Jeremy hadn't said anything to Angie about last night.

Angie and I scoured the cupboards looking for food for breakfast. All we could find to eat was the unflavored oatmeal and the pitcher of milk in the refrigerator. I poured myself a mug of the milk. It didn't look like normal milk coming out of the pitcher.

"What's wrong with this stuff?" I said. I held the mug up to my nose and sniffed. It didn't smell sour.

"That must be raw milk," Angie said looking

over my shoulder.

"Raw milk?" I said. "What's raw milk?"

"You know, it hasn't been pasteurized or homogenized or whatever they do to it before it ends up at the supermarket."

"You mean this is the way it is when it comes directly from the cow?" I asked.

"Something like that," Angie said.

I wasn't sure what she meant by "something like that," but I lifted the mug to my lips and took a cautious sip.

It was nothing like the milk in our refrigerator back home, but it wasn't bad. I gulped down half the mug and filled it to the top again. I put the pitcher on the kitchen table.

Angie boiled some water and we found three chipped, white bowls for the oatmeal. I was filling the bowls with oats when Jeremy came in the kitchen door grinning at me—like he wanted to remind me about last night without saying anything out loud. He sat down at the table. When he saw what we were having for breakfast he made a face.

"This is the best you could find?" he asked.

I nodded.

"I thought farmers ate big breakfasts of bacon and eggs every morning," he said. "That's what they always do in movies."

I filled a mug with milk and slid it in front of Jeremy.

Jeremy raised a spoonful of lumpy oatmeal to his lips and put a little in his mouth. He made another face.

I smiled at him and took a big gulp of milk.

"It's like sawdust," Jeremy complained. "Isn't there any jam or something we can mix in with this?"

"How about some green beans and yogurt?" Angie suggested. Jeremy winced and then tried another taste of oatmeal. I finished off my mug of milk and poured some more from the pitcher.

"Didn't your mom say there was a general store somewhere near here?" Angie asked.

"Yeah," I said. "She said there's a store a couple of miles down the road." I took another sip of milk.

"Who's got money?" Angie asked. "I don't want to starve to death. Let's go buy some groceries for the week. I'm sure our folks will give us the money back when we get back home."

I wiped milk from my lips with the back of my wrist and looked over at Jeremy. He was shaking his head. "If *you* guys want to spend your money on groceries, be my guest," he said. "I can make do with what we've got here. I'm not picky."

Jeremy filled his mouth with a big spoonful of oatmeal and tried to swallow. He started coughing. He grabbed his mug and washed the oatmeal down with a gulp of milk. He took another gulp of milk and then looked down into the mug as if the milk had a funny taste.

"You *do* know that's goat's milk don't you?" Angie asked.

Jeremy spewed the milk back into his mug. "Goat's milk?" he said. "You sure?"

I suddenly felt queasy.

"You didn't see any *cows* out back did you?" Angie asked. "Why do you think he keeps that old goat?"

Jeremy ran over to the sink and rinsed his mouth out with tap water. As he walked back to the table he pulled his wallet out of his back pocket and slapped a ten dollar bill on the table in front of Angie.

"I guess you two are going for groceries," he said. "Just do me a favor—see if the supermarket has a copy of this month's *Skateboarder* magazine."

The highway was perfectly straight and level. I coasted out onto it from Uncle Allen's drive, with my empty backpack on my shoulders. I tried to memorize how this stretch of road looked, so we'd be able to find it again on our way home. Angie and I started to pedal.

The road was easy to ride on—it was perfectly level—but as we passed field after identical field, it was hard to believe we were making any progress. Every once in a while a car or a truck would rocket past us and disappear over the horizon, leaving us wobbling at the side of the road in its dust. I thought we'd never get there.

When we got to the general store, we almost rode right by it. It didn't look like any store I'd ever seen. I'd been expecting something like the supermarkets we have back home in the city, but this was really just a big house—like Uncle Allen's, but closer to the road. A few pickup trucks were parked on the dirt out front and a big sign read:

GROCERIES–PARTS–FEED.

"This must be it," Angie said.

She coasted off the highway and rolled across the dirt parking area raising a cloud of red dust behind her. I followed her and we leaned our bikes against the front porch railing. I followed Angie up the steps. The porch was lined with open crates and barrels full of potatoes, broccoli, and ears of corn.

Inside, the store was dark and smelled like a lumber yard. The wooden floor felt gritty underfoot. I stood just inside the door a minute and let my eyes adjust to the darkness. Angie picked up a basket from a rack near the door and began looking around. She disappeared down a row of shelves.

The whole downstairs of the store was one big room with a counter that ran all the way around. In the middle was a maze of shelves and racks, crowded with everything a person could possibly need.

I walked around and looked at some of the stuff for sale. The store not only had groceries but hardware and auto parts and everything else a farmer might want to buy.

There was only one other customer in the store—a tall, thin man wearing a cowboy hat. The store was very quiet. It seemed like the kind of hushed place where people whisper to each other—like a library.

I made my way down one of the aisles. The floorboards groaned sometimes when I took a step.

I passed a shelf of kerosene lamps and candles and found a rack of different kinds of flashlights. Now *that* was something that would be useful in Uncle Allen's dark house. I sorted through all of them and picked a small one I could afford, then I went to look for batteries.

In my search I came upon a wide rack crammed

full of newspapers and magazines, and I remembered that Jeremy had asked us to get him a copy of *Skateboarder* magazine. I knew the chances were slim that I'd find a copy—how many farmers have time to skateboard?—but I thought I'd look through the rack so I could tell Jeremy I'd tried.

The top shelves were crammed with newspapers, almanacs, and farming magazines. The man in the cowboy hat came over and stood in the next aisle. He picked up a pot and studied it. I flipped past *Field and Stream* and *Popular Mechanics*, and after a few minutes I'd looked at every magazine on the top shelf.

I kneeled down on the wooden floor so I could go through the lower racks. I started at the back. They didn't seem to have more than one copy of anything, and some were more than a year old.

They were in no particular order. *Home Decorating Monthly* was next to *Harley Davidson* magazine, which was right next to *Home Stereo Consumer*. I flipped through magazine after magazine until a certain magazine caught my eye: *Alien Encounters*.

I tugged it out from among the others. On the cover was a picture of a farmer in a field at night, holding a pitchfork. Hovering in the air in front of him was a huge spaceship with three glowing lights on the underside. I felt my stomach clench suddenly. I held the magazine close and studied the cover. It was a painting, not a photograph—but it was still enough to give me the shivers.

I opened the magazine and thumbed through the pages. It had dozens of blurry pictures of flying saucers. It was full of articles like "Crop Circles: The True Story" and "The Glenfield UFO Cover-Up." Most of the photos looked fake—like someone had thrown a hubcap up in the air and snapped a picture. I was studying a picture of the Glenfield UFO—it looked like a clump of mylar balloons to me—when I heard a voice on the other side of the shelves.

"Howdy, Bob," the voice said softly. "How are things going out your way?"

"Holding our own," mumbled the man in the cowboy hat.

I flipped through a few more pages of the UFO magazine and ignored the two farmers talking on the other side of the shelf. I was looking at an article called "Aliens Among Us," when one of the farmers whispered, "You see all the activity last night?"

I stopped reading. I held my breath and listened.

"Yeah," the other farmer answered softly. "Another few nights like that and we'll be rid of every last one of them. I can't wait till this invasion is over."

I tried to hold myself still, but I was suddenly shaking.

"They were a lot harder to get rid of this time, weren't they?" one of the farmers whispered. "It's not an easy job to do at night."

"Sure enough," the other said softly. "But they've been here a lot longer than we have. They know all the good hiding places. Getting them at night is our only chance."

"Well I'm not going to rest until every last one of them is gone."

"You got that right."

I heard the shuffle of feet on the other side of the magazine rack. The two farmers wandered down the aisle. I could no longer make out what they were whispering.

My heart pounded. I slipped the open UFO magazine to the ground beside me and quietly rose up on my feet. I peeked over the top of the magazine rack into the next aisle. The two farmers stood at the far end. They were both skinny. The one without a cowboy hat was perfectly bald—just like Uncle Allen. They stood in front of a rack of knives. The bald one tested a knife edge with a long, bony finger.

I ducked back down. They hadn't seen me. I noticed the open magazine at my feet, and my stomach lurched again. ALIENS AMONG US, the headline said. Beneath the headline it asked: IS YOUR NEIGHBOR FROM OUTER SPACE?

I looked back at the two farmers. Was it my imagination, or did these two men have the same grayish tint to their skin as Uncle Allen?

I picked the magazine off the floor, rolled it up and tucked it under my arm. I ducked down low, so the two "farmers" couldn't see me and went off searching frantically for Angie.

Chapter 9

A re you OK?" Angie asked when we had cycled a few minutes in silence. She pulled up next to me on her bike. "You're acting kind of weird."

I glanced behind us at the general store on the distant horizon. "I'm OK," I told her. My shoulders ached from my heavy backpack, now crammed full of cans.

Angie coasted next to me for a minute, studying me. I stared ahead at the straight asphalt road. I was still feeling shaky from the conversation I'd overheard.

"Why did you want to buy that dumb flying saucer magazine?" Angie asked. She glanced behind her to make sure no traffic was coming up behind us.

"I don't know," I said, feeling myself blush. "I just did."

"You kept staring at those two old farmers in the store," she said. "What was *that* all about? Is there something you're not telling me?"

Angie glanced behind us again and then put on her brakes and fell behind me into single file to let a yellow pickup pass by. She pedaled to catch up to me again.

"Wasn't that one of them?" Angie asked, puffing a little.

"One of what?" I asked.

"One of those two old farmers from the store," she said. "He was driving that truck."

I looked at the yellow truck, which was now far ahead of us on the highway.

"So?" I said.

"I don't know," Angie said. "The way you kept watching them—I thought maybe you knew them from somewhere."

"No," I said. "I've never seen them before in my life."

"I didn't think so," Angie said. "We're a long way from home."

Not nearly as far from home as that guy is, I thought. I looked ahead of us at the truck. It was almost out of sight.

"Say," I asked, trying to sound casual. "You didn't see what those men had in their baskets, did you? Did you notice what they were buying?"

"Yeah," Angie said. "They were buying lemon yogurt and string beans."

I gave a little jump, and my bike wobbled off the road and onto the dirt shoulder. I put on the brakes and steered back onto the blacktop.

"That's what they were buying?" I asked, feeling the blood drain from my face. "You're sure?"

Angie shook her head. "I was joking," she said, coasting beside me. "I have no idea what they were buying. What's the matter with you?"

"Nothing," I told her. "Everything's fine."

When we got home, we found Jeremy dozing in the porch swing.

"We do all the work," Angie said, "and he takes a nap."

"I don't think he got much sleep last night," I told her.

I nudged Jeremy awake.

"It's about *time* you guys got back," he said yawning. "I'm bored to death out here on my own. No television. No radio. Not even a phone to make crank calls." Jeremy sat up on the porch swing and stretched. Half his face was red from sleeping on it.

"You mean you didn't enjoy your time alone with Uncle Allen?" Angie teased. "The two of you have so much in common."

"Yeah," Jeremy joked. "We played a little hockey in the kitchen, until he had to leave."

Angie opened the door and headed inside with her backpack full of groceries. I stayed on the porch with Jeremy, my heavy backpack slung over one shoulder.

"Uncle Allen left?" I asked. "But his truck's parked around the side of the house. I saw it when we were coming up the drive."

"Someone came and picked him up," Jeremy told me. "Could have been his twin brother, they looked so much a like. Uncle Allen said he won't be back till really late."

I looked back along the dirt drive that led to the highway. "The guy who came for Uncle Allen," I said, "was he driving a yellow pickup?"

"Sure was," Jeremy said yawning. "How did you know that?"

For dinner we ate well. We boiled spaghetti noodles and dumped a large can of chili over the top with some melted cheese. I didn't realize how hungry I was.

After dinner, we went upstairs to Jeremy's room again. None of us wanted to be downstairs when Uncle Allen came home. Even up on the third floor it was hard to relax, knowing that he might come through the door at any moment.

When the sun started to go down we shut all the windows in the house, though it was even hotter than last night. We didn't want Uncle Allen to have any reason to come upstairs looking for us when he got home.

I lounged on the mattress, reading my UFO magazine. Jeremy was laying out a game of solitaire on the floor, and Angie was standing at the window looking out. I read the cover story about a farmer who saw three glowing lights above his field. The police said the lights were swamp gas. I didn't know what swamp gas was, but I was willing to take their word for it.

"Man, is it ever hot," Jeremy said.

"Don't complain," Angie said. "It's even hotter in my room. It's on the south side, and it's got those big windows."

"Pick another room," Jeremy said. "There's only about four hundred in this crazy house."

"Ryan has the best one," Angie said.

I looked up from my magazine.

"It's on the north side of the house," she explained. "It doesn't get as much light during the day."

"If you want my room, you can have it," I told her.

"What'll *you* do?"

"I can sleep in here with Jeremy," I said.

Jeremy grinned at me. He knew I didn't want to be alone in that room again. I hoped he wouldn't say anything to Angie.

"OK by me," he said. "We can do each other's hair."

Angie went downstairs to move her stuff to my room.

"Is *that* why you bought that magazine?" Jeremy asked once she was gone. "You don't still think you saw a UFO last night, do you?"

I looked at my magazine. It was open to a picture of a UFO hovering over a Winnebego. To me it looked more like a blurry photo of a streetlight taken through the trees.

"I don't know what I think," I admitted.

I was half-reading an article called "The Night I Was Abducted." I know I shouldn't have been—it was the last thing I needed.

The article was by a woman named Harriet Schecter from New Jersey. She claimed that aliens took her on their ship and performed experiments on her. It was hard not to laugh. All the articles in the magazine were pretty nutty, but this one was even more stupid than the rest.

I was beginning to relax—the more I looked at the magazine, the more convinced I was that UFOs couldn't possibly exist.

I had just arrived at the part where Harriet Schecter's door flew open and she saw a group of tiny gray men standing on her front porch. At that moment, the door to Jeremy's room suddenly burst open and the door handle ricocheted off the wall.

I was on my feet and sprinting toward the window before I realized it was only Angie. She'd kicked open the door because her arms were full with my back pack and sleeping bag.

I closed the curtain, as though that was why I'd gotten up—as though I hadn't nearly dove through the window to escape from some aliens. I don't think I fooled anyone. When I turned back around, Angie and Jeremy were both staring at me. I tried to smile at them. "So who's up for some hangman?" I asked.

Around midnight Jeremy's room began to cool down, and I drifted off to sleep. I'd closed and locked the door as soon as Jeremy started snoring.

I wanted to make sure that no one could sneak into the room while we were asleep. Too many people had burst through that door already.

I lay on my back and looked at the ceiling for a while and then rolled over on my side. I could tell I was going to have a hard time getting to sleep.

I tried to relax. I tried to get my mind to hold still, but there was just no way. I kept thinking about the lights in the sky and the farmer in the yellow truck. My mind kept straying to Dylan's picture of the flying saucer and weird old Uncle Allen.

I knew there was a simple explanation for everything, but the more I lay awake, trying to put all the pieces together in different ways, the more tense I got.

I thought about the verses I'd read in the family Bible:

> If I say, Surely the darkness shall cover
>   me;
> even the night shall be light about me.
> Yea, the darkness hideth not from thee;
> but the night shineth as the day;
> the darkness and the light are both alike
>   to thee.

It was nice to think that God might be watching

over me—that He was with me even now. I thought about how nice it would be to be able to take my problems to God, instead of worrying and trying to sort things out on my own. But I didn't know how to do that. I was too wrapped up in myself to think of anything other than me. I rolled over onto my stomach and tried to put all the pieces together again, looking for an answer.

I was only asleep a few minutes when a frantic banging on the door awakened me. I sat straight up and looked at the door. Everything was silent again. I glanced over at Jeremy. He rolled over on the mattress but didn't wake up. Everything was silent.

The banging began again, more furious than before. I scrambled out of my sleeping bag and stood in the middle of the room, looking frantically around me for something I could use as a weapon. My heart pounded. All I could think about was Harriet Schecter of New Jersey and all those little gray men on her front step. I was terrified. I wanted to say "Who's there?" but for some reason my mouth couldn't form the words.

"Let me in!" a high voice insisted. *"Open this thing up!"*

In my confusion, it occurred to me that for aliens, they spoke English very well.

"You guys, I *saw* something," the voice said. "Let me *in!*"

It was Angie.

I blew out the breath I'd been holding and went to the door.

"You'll never believe it," she said when I pulled open the door. "You'll never believe what I saw." She pushed past me into the room.

"Don't tell me," Jeremy said groggily, propping himself up on his elbows on the mattress. "You saw a UFO."

Angie reached over and switched on the light. All of us were blinded for a second. "How did you know that?" she asked, staring down at Jeremy.

"Because this knucklehead woke me up in the middle of the night *last* night," Jeremy told her. "You're both out of your minds."

"You don't believe me?" Angie sputtered, her hands on her hips.

"I'm saying I don't believe in UFOs," Jeremy said, rubbing his eyes. "And neither do you."

"But I *saw* it," Angie insisted. "I saw it with my own two eyes."

"What did you see?" I asked her, sitting down on the mattress next to Jeremy.

"This . . . *thing* . . . came down from the sky," she said. "I rolled over in bed and looked out the window, and these lights zoomed down and disappeared behind the trees."

"Three of them?" I asked.

"Yeah, I think so," she said. "So I got up and went to the window, and about a minute later they zoomed back up in the sky again."

"*See*," I told Jeremy. "I'm not crazy. She saw it too." I don't know *why* I felt happy—I'd have been a lot better off if it *wasn't* true.

"You're *both* crazy," Jeremy said.

"But we both saw the same thing," I insisted. "How come she said she saw three lights—just like I did? I didn't tell her what I saw last night."

Angie looked at me angrily. "You mean you saw that thing out there and you didn't tell me?" she shouted. "You let me sleep in that room by myself?"

"Shhhh," I told her. "Calm down. You'll wake Uncle Allen."

"He's not home yet," Angie shouted. "I can yell all I want."

"Both of you be quiet," Jeremy said. Angie and I both looked at him. He was holding up my UFO magazine. On the cover was the picture of the farmer with the pitchfork and the flying saucer with three bright lights.

"Does this look familiar?" Jeremy asked. "This stupid magazine is enough to give anyone nightmares."

Angie looked at the magazine. I could tell she was thinking it over.

"OK," I said. "But that doesn't explain what *I* saw. I didn't *have* the magazine last night."

"I don't know," Jeremy said. "Maybe you were dreaming too, or maybe it was just a reflection on the glass. It could have been hundreds of things, but it wasn't a UFO."

Jeremy looked back and forth from me to Angie. Angie sat down on the mattress so we were all in a circle. She looked like she was calming down.

"Look," Jeremy said. "Why would a UFO come all the way to planet Earth, only to land in the middle of nowhere—and then take off a minute later?"

It was a good question. I shrugged my shoulders and looked at Angie.

"I don't know," she said defensively. "Maybe they were dropping something off."

Jeremy started laughing. "Yeah, right! Maybe they were delivering pizza!" he said. "What in the world would they be dropping off way out here in the middle of nowhere?"

After his question, a silence hung in the air. And then we heard the unmistakable sound of footsteps coming up the front steps to the porch.

I jumped up and ran to the window. I peeked out between the curtains. Down in the shadows I saw Uncle Allen cross the porch to the front door. I looked up to see if there was a pickup truck turning out onto the highway.

There wasn't a car in sight.

Chapter 10

"Y ou can't be serious," Jeremy told me. "Uncle Allen is *not* an alien, and he's not going to abduct us and take us to another planet."

I paced back and forth. I couldn't sit still. "Well then *you* explain it," I said hotly. "*You* explain what those two farmers were talking about—'I can't wait till this invasion is over.' Those were their exact words."

"I don't know what they were talking about," Jeremy admitted. "I wasn't there. But I *do* know they weren't aliens—they were just a couple of old farmers."

I looked over at Angie. She sat on the mattress with her back against the wall, hugging her knees. It was clear she didn't want to be a part of this argument.

"Angie and I *both* saw their ship," I said trying not to raise my voice. "It just dropped off Uncle Allen. What more proof do you want?"

"Will you *listen* to yourself?" Jeremy said. "This is insane. That stupid magazine has turned your brain to mush."

"Why doesn't Uncle Allen want us to go outside at night?" I challenged him. "Why doesn't he eat normal food? It's because he *isn't* really human."

"Elvis Presley ate deep-fried peanut butter and banana sandwiches," Jeremy pointed out. "That didn't make him an alien." Jeremy's eyes grew suddenly wide in mock terror. He leaned in close. "Or maybe Elvis *is* an alien," he said. "I'll bet *he's* the one behind all this. He'll probably burst in here any minute in a sequined jumpsuit and whisk us all away to Jupiter."

"You're not funny, Jeremy," I said coldly. "We could be in some real danger here."

"We're only in danger of having you two go off the deep end," he said. "Just think a minute about what you're saying here. Just take a minute and think of how crazy you sound."

I was angry. I didn't like being called a nut, but I also didn't like arguing with my brother. I took a few deep breaths and tried to calm down. "I wish you'd believe me, Jeremy," I said, frustrated. "I really *did* see something fly up into the sky."

Jeremy shook his head. He was as frustrated as I was. "Look, how can I convince you that there isn't a UFO out there?" he said. "What can I do to prove that this is just some big misunderstanding?"

"We can all go out there tonight and see what's going on," Angie said.

We both looked at her suddenly. She'd been so quiet, I'd forgotten she was there.

"It's the only way we'll know for sure," Angie said.

"I'm in," Jeremy said. "Let's give Uncle Allen time to fall asleep and we'll go."

I felt a sudden flutter of fear in my stomach. Angie and Jeremy both looked at me. I tried to think of some excuse not to do what Angie was suggesting. "Uncle Allen told us not to go outside at night," I croaked. "Remember? He said if we knew what was good for us we'd stay inside."

"If Uncle Allen is a Martian who's plotting to kidnap us," Jeremy pointed out, "why in the world do you want to do what he tells you?"

It was a good point, and I couldn't think of what to say in return. I stood there in the middle of the room, nervous and speechless. I felt drops of sweat creep down my sides under my shirt.

Angie looked up at me. "Come on, Ryan," she said. "I'm scared too, but we've got to find out what's going on around here."

We kept the lights off and spoke in whispers. When we weren't talking, I could hear the other two breathing softly in the dark; and I could hear the old house creak and settle. I kept thinking of the verses I'd read in the old family Bible.

I crawled quietly over next to Angie. "Hey, Angie," I whispered. "You read the Bible a lot. What does it say about this kind of thing?"

"I've been thinking about that," she said. "I don't know if it says anything about other planets and that kind of stuff, and we've never talked about it in church. I guess it *might* be possible—God could make other worlds if He wanted to—after all, He *is* God."

"Well, if there *might* be a UFO out there, why are we going to look for it?"

"Because it's the only way we'll know for sure," Angie said. "Don't you want to know?"

"Sure," I said. "But—" I couldn't think of how to finish the sentence.

"You're scared," Angie whispered. "I am too."

"Well then why do you want to go outside?"

"People are afraid of what they don't understand," Angie said. "I guess that's natural. But God understands everything. He knows what's out there, and He can protect us."

"'Yea, the darkness hideth not from thee; but the night shineth as the day: the darkness and the light are both alike to thee.'" I quoted.

"Where did you learn that?" Angie asked.

"I read it in Uncle Allen's family Bible last night," I told her. "I've been thinking about it a lot."

"That's great," Angie said. "And it's exactly what I mean. I might be scared because I don't know what's going to happen, but deep down I know that God's got everything under control. He sees and knows everything, and He's on my side."

"That's OK for you," I said. "God *likes* you. You go to church and all that kind of stuff."

"You're wrong," Angie said. "God *loves* me. And He loves you just as much. He's willing to help you. All you have to do is ask."

We fell silent for a while. Even though it was dark, I closed my eyes. I'd never prayed before, so I wasn't sure how to do it; and I was a little embarrassed. But there in the dark I told God that I wanted to know more about Him and that I hoped He'd look out for me and Jeremy tonight, the same way He looked out for Angie.

Chapter 11

O K," Jeremy whispered about an hour later. "I think it's safe. Uncle Allen's got to be asleep by now."

Jeremy rose to his feet in the darkness. Angie and I sat where we were a few seconds longer—I think we were both saying last-minute prayers.

When I did stand up, I could feel my heart pounding and my fingers tingled. I heard Angie push herself up from the floor and stand.

"Switch on the flashlight," Jeremy told me softly. I fished the tiny flashlight I had bought at the general store from my pocket and switched it on. We had agreed not to turn on any of the house lights— we didn't want anyone to know we were up. I shone the dim circle of light at our feet. Its orange glow lit Angie and Jeremy's faces eerily. Jeremy unlocked the door quietly and pulled it open.

My flashlight was too small to illuminate the whole length of the hallway, so we shuffled softly along the wooden floor past closed doors, pushing back the darkness with our dim light as we moved. It felt for all the world like the old house was listening.

The end of the hallway came into view. When we got to the top step, I shined the small light down the twisting black stairway.

"Lead the way," Jeremy whispered. "You've got the flashlight."

I stood for a moment looking down into the shadows of the stairway; it was like looking down a dark well. I didn't want to go first, but I didn't want to give up the flashlight either.

"Let's go," Jeremy whispered.

I took a deep breath and started down the steps, the beam of the flashlight shaking. There was no way to see more than a few steps ahead. I paused on each step until I felt Angie on the step behind me. Finally the second-floor hallway came into view.

When we all reached the second floor safely, I shone the light in the open doorway to the room where Angie and I had both seen the lights in the sky. "Let's just see if the lights are still there," I said. I was hoping Jeremy would see them himself, and then we wouldn't have to go outside.

I stepped into the doorway and shined my light at the glass door to the balcony. Suddenly a bright light appeared in the window. I dropped the flashlight. It hit the floor with a loud crack, and suddenly we were plunged into darkness.

"It was just a *reflection*, you spaz," Jeremy whispered. "It was just your flashlight."

I bent and picked up the flashlight. I switched it off and on with my thumb. Nothing happened. Panic rose in me—I sure didn't want to go outside tonight without even a flashlight.

Please, Lord, I pleaded silently. *Please let it work*. I unscrewed the top of the flashlight and rattled the batteries inside. I twisted the top back in place, and suddenly the light came on. It shocked me so much I dropped it again.

It stayed lit this time when it hit the ground, but it rolled loudly across the hallway floor, lighting up the planks of wood as it went.

"Shhh," Angie said. "Can't you hang on to that thing?"

"I'm doing my best," I whispered, retrieving the flashlight from the floor. "I'm just a bit tense tonight, OK? It isn't often I get abducted by aliens."

"OK," she whispered back. "Just keep it down. We don't want everyone to know we're up."

Everyone? I thought. Why did she have to use that word? How many people—or things—might be waiting for us out there? I imagined dark creatures watching the house from the grove of trees—seeing our flashlight flicker in each window as we passed. I shivered.

We started slowly down the second-floor hallway. Uncle Allen's room was somewhere below us, but we weren't sure where, so we froze and held our breath every time a floorboard creaked. It seemed like an hour before the stairway to the first floor came into view.

We all gathered at the top step, and I shined the flashlight down the stairway. This staircase didn't curve around like the other, so we could see all the way to the front hallway. Even the front door was dimly lit.

Jeremy started down the staircase first. These stairs were so creaky, we knew we'd have to go down them one at a time. I stood at the top holding the flashlight. Angie stood so close to me that I could feel her breath on my neck.

Jeremy moved slowly, step by step, holding the banister. He was about halfway down when he lowered his foot to a new step. The step gave a loud groan when he put his weight on it. The noise seemed to echo through the house. We all froze.

Something moved below us on the first floor. Maybe it was a door opening. Maybe it was just Uncle Allen sitting up in bed. I couldn't tell. Jeremy looked up at us, fear in his eyes.

I switched the flashlight off, and we were plunged into utter blackness again. Angie pressed against me. We all strained our ears, listening. We stood that way for several long minutes, frozen in silence. Nothing moved in the dark house.

I switched the flashlight back on. Jeremy still stood on the same step, hugging the banister, looking pale. He looked up at me and nodded. He pointed at the step he was standing on—the seventh—as if to warn Angie and me to avoid stepping on it, then he completed his slow journey down the stairs.

Angie was next. When she got to the sixth step, she turned and gripped the banister with both hands. She slowly lowered herself backwards over the seventh step to the one below. When she had safely passed the creaking step, she smiled up at me. Then she turned and deftly stepped down the last few steps without a sound.

Now it was my turn. I slowly lowered myself from step to step, pointing the flashlight ahead of me. I kept my eyes fixed on the seventh step, so I wouldn't lose track of it. I stopped on the sixth step. At that point it occurred to me that I couldn't grip the banister with both hands the way Angie had, because I was holding the flashlight.

I wiped my empty left hand on my jeans and gripped the banister. I swung my foot out beyond the seventh step and tried to lower myself to the one below it. As I did, my hand slipped, and I fell into empty space. My stomach twisted. I tumbled noisily down the last few steps and hit the first floor on my back with a loud thud.

I was stunned. The wind was completely knocked out of me. While I struggled to breathe, I frantically felt beside me on the floor for the flashlight and switched it off.

I lay in the darkness listening, my knees and elbows throbbing from my tumble down the stairs. I heard a creak somewhere in the back of the house, and then footsteps. Angie and Jeremy's footsteps shuffled across the floor into the parlor. A door opened and a shaft of light appeared in the back hallway. I had no time to follow the others. I scrambled on hands and knees beneath the heavy wooden table against the hallway wall.

I squeezed myself into a ball as the footsteps came along the hallway toward me. I pressed myself against the wall.

The footsteps stopped at the foot of the stairs. I turned my head and peeked out from under the table. Uncle Allen's large bare feet faced the staircase. I knew he was looking up, listening for us. I held my breath. My heart was pounding so hard I worried that Uncle Allen might be able to hear it.

Uncle Allen walked to the front door and unlocked it. He pulled the door open. In the dim light from his open bedroom door, I could see him standing, looking up at the night sky. I eased myself backward so he wouldn't see me under the table when he turned around.

After a long moment, he sighed and pushed the door shut. He walked past me, and his footsteps moved along the back hallway. When his door clicked shut, the house fell into darkness once again.

I didn't dare move until I heard Angie and Jeremy tiptoe back into the front hall, and then I crawled out from under the table. I lit the flashlight again. Angie and Jeremy looked much paler now. I pointed the flashlight at the stairway. It was too dangerous to go back up—there was no way we could sneak back to Jeremy's room now that Uncle Allen was awake.

I pointed the flashlight at the front door. It was like we all knew what the others were thinking. We tiptoed to the front door, and Jeremy slowly twisted back the lock.

"Turn off the flashlight," Jeremy whispered.

I did.

Jeremy twisted the doorknob and pulled the door open a crack. He peeked out. After a few seconds he pulled it wider and stuck his head out. Standing behind him, I felt the cool night air on my face.

Jeremy stepped back and pulled the door wide enough so we could slip through. In a moment we were all standing on the dark porch under the millions of bright stars that crowded the sky. The stars shone so brightly, it seemed like you could hear them buzzing. I looked up at the sky and wondered which star Uncle Allen called home.

I made sure the door wasn't locked this time when I pulled it shut behind us. We stood a moment on the edge of the porch steps, watching the trees for movement. Choruses of crickets chirped in rhythm all around us.

We crept down the steps. Angie and I followed Jeremy across the starlit grass toward the black shapes of the trees. As we moved, the crickets in front of us fell silent until we passed.

When we got close to the trees, Jeremy stopped.

"I guess we can turn on the flashlight," he said. "What do you think?"

I put my thumb on the flashlight's switch, but I didn't turn it on. I didn't know what to do.

"Won't that make us easier to see?" Angie asked.

Jeremy let out a nervous laugh. "There's nothing out here to see us," he said, but there was doubt in his voice.

"Why don't we save the batteries," I said. "In case we need the flashlight later."

"OK," he said. "But let's stick together."

I slipped the light into my pocket.

As we moved among the dark trees, I held one hand out in front of me so I could touch Jeremy's tee shirt. I held my other hand in front of my face— there were all kinds of low branches and twigs in among these tangled trees. Angie walked behind me with her hand on my shoulder.

The ground felt soggy, and a couple of times I nearly tripped on some tree roots. I was about to suggest that we turn on the flashlight, when Jeremy suddenly said, "Here we are."

I looked up. We had reached the other side of the grove of trees. Stretched out before us was the dark field where Angie and I had seen the lights in the sky. Black rows of bushes covered the field. It was impossible to tell what was growing there.

Above the field the sky stretched to the horizon, glittering with stars.

No one spoke. Our tiny group stood there looking out across the vast field. We might have been standing on the edge of the ocean, the field looked so huge.

Now that we were here, it didn't seem as sinister as I had expected. Crickets chirped reassuringly all around us in the darkness.

"I don't see any flying saucers," Jeremy said. "Do you?"

I hated to admit it, but I was beginning to think Jeremy was right. There was nothing unusual about this field. The strange thing was that I was kind of disappointed.

"What's that smell?" Angie asked.

I sniffed. Something smelled faintly like fumes.

"What smell?" Jeremy said. "I don't smell anything."

I stepped down into the field and sniffed again. The smell was a little stronger there. Maybe the smell had something to do with the lights.

"Where are you going?" Jeremy called after me. He sounded nervous—he was the oldest one there, and I knew he felt responsible. "Come back here."

"I'm not going *anywhere*," I said. "I just want to find that smell. Maybe it's swamp gas—whatever that is."

I pulled the flashlight from my pocket. I switched it on and took a few steps farther into the field between the rows of bushes. The smell was growing stronger.

"I don't know what you're talking about," Jeremy whispered urgently. "I don't smell anything. Come back over here."

The bushes were as high as my shoulders. I pointed the flashlight in front of me and took a few more steps between the rows. My heart jackhammered away, but I knew I had to get to the bottom of this. I took a couple more steps and stopped. This was as far as I wanted to go.

I pointed my flashlight around among the bushes. A mist seemed to swirl around the bushes in places—but it was much too hot and dry a night for mist. It didn't make sense, and now the smell was stronger than ever—it felt like it was burning my nose and lips.

"There's something weird going on out here," I said.

"R-Ryan," Angie stammered. "Ryan, look!"

I turned and shone my flashlight at Angie. I could dimly see her pointing across the huge field behind me. She looked terrified.

"Someone's driving through the field," she said.

I turned and saw a pair of headlights tearing across the field toward us. I dropped the flashlight.

My mouth fell open. It looked like a huge pickup truck was plowing across the rows of bushes toward me at a hundred miles an hour. I was seeing it, but it was impossible!

"Run!" Angie yelled. "Hide in the trees."

I dropped to my knees and felt around on the soil for my flashlight. My hands scrambled around on the dirt. The lights swept across the field. They were blinding.

"Run!" Jeremy yelled.

I turned and stumbled toward his voice. The lights coming up behind me scattered weird flickering shadows ahead of me. As the truck came closer, I could hear the sputtering hum of its engine. It didn't sound like any pickup truck I'd ever heard before. I scrambled and stumbled across the uneven ground. It was hard to tell the bushes from the writhing shadows. I couldn't see where I was going.

I glanced over my shoulder. The lights pursued me like they were hunting me down. It was no truck. *The lights were ten feet off the ground!*

I ran, tumbling and scrambling over the bushes, tripping and tearing my clothes as I went. I heard Angie's terrified scream. I heard Jeremy shouting.

My foot tripped on something, and I tumbled blindly through the bushes. I landed on my back, snared and tangled by the bushes. The lights zoomed forward. I clenched my fists and cried out, "Help me, Lord!"

The humming sound became a roar. The lights were on me now, blindingly bright. A loud hissing noise drowned out all other sounds. At the moment the lights came directly over me they rocketed straight up in the air. I coughed and sputtered. My eyes stung. My lungs burned. My head swirled.

I thought I was drowning. Water was splashing in my face and on my body, like I had fallen beneath a waterfall and couldn't move. I seemed to be dreaming. All kinds of thoughts and pictures swirled through my head. I saw Dylan hand me the picture of the flying saucer through the Jeep's window. I heard the farmer's voice: "Another few nights like that and we'll be rid of every last one of them." I imagined Mrs. Harriet Schecter of New Jersey lying on a table in a flying saucer while a crowd of gray aliens did experiments on her.

I felt like I was moving. I couldn't open my eyes or move—but I felt like I was strapped into a seat, and the seat was speeding through space. I struggled to open my eyes, but it was like they were glued shut. I couldn't seem to work my arms or legs.

I prayed for God's strength. I concentrated. I groaned. It took all my energy, but I managed to peel open my stinging eyes. Everything was blurry. Lights seemed to flash by me on every side as I hurtled through space. I turned my head. I saw a blurry figure beside me. Lights flickered across its large, gray face. I tried to focus. I strained to see clearly. My head was spinning.

Just before I lost consciousness again, I recognized the face—*Uncle Allen*!

Chapter 12

I don't know how long I was asleep. The next thing I saw was a blinding white light. I was lying on my back on some kind of bed, and a bright light was shining down on me. I couldn't see clearly, but everything around me was white. A large face loomed above me—I couldn't be sure, but it looked like the farmer in the yellow pickup truck—another alien! *It all made sense now!*

I blinked and tried to focus. My ears rang. The alien's lips moved, but I couldn't hear what he was saying.

In a moment another face appeared above me. I stared at it until it came into focus. It was Uncle Allen. My stomach dropped. *It was all true!* I had been abducted by aliens, and they had me in their ship! They were doing experiments on me, just like they did on Harriet Schecter of New Jersey!

I noticed two more faces looking down at me. They were smaller. I struggled to see them clearly. It was Jeremy and Angie.

"Oh no!" I moaned. "The aliens got you too!"

"He spoke!" Uncle Allen said. "What did he say?"

"Something about aliens," the other alien told him. "He's delirious."

I struggled to sit up and felt arms behind me helping. I looked around the spaceship. A curtain hung from the ceiling. There was a television on the wall. Somehow this wasn't what I expected the inside of a flying saucer to look like. My eyes burned, but my head was clearing.

"Where am I?" I asked.

"The hospital," Angie told me. "You're in the hospital. Don't you remember?"

"Remember what?"

"The crop duster," she said. "All of us washing you off with the hose. The ride over here in Uncle Allen's truck. You don't remember any of it?"

"Huh?" I said. My head was throbbing.

"You got sprayed by a crop duster," Jeremy explained. "You passed out."

"I *warned* you kids not to go outside after dark," Uncle Allen said. "That's when the citrus bugs come out. They were spraying some pretty strong stuff out there tonight. It's the worst invasion of the things we've ever seen in these parts."

"Another few nights like tonight and we'll be rid of every last one of them," the other man said.

I looked at him. "Who are *you?*" I asked.

"That's Mr. Grant," Uncle Allen said. "He owns the field you were in when you got sprayed."

"He drove me and Jeremy out here in his truck," Angie said. "We were all worried sick about you."

"There wasn't a spaceship?" I asked, still confused.

"Spaceship?" Uncle Allen said. "He *is* delirious."

"I think he's OK," Angie told them. "It's kind of a game we were all playing."

The doctor wanted to keep me overnight, just to keep an eye on me. When they were sure I was OK, Uncle Allen, Mr. Grant, Jeremy, and Angie got ready to leave, so I could get some sleep. Uncle Allen walked Mr. Grant out to his truck. Angie and Jeremy stayed with me.

Angie picked her backpack up from the floor and opened it. She pulled out my toothbrush, my comb and a change of clothes and put them on my bedside table. "I thought you'd be needing these," she said.

"This isn't fair," Jeremy told me. "You get television and air conditioning—why couldn't *I* have been sprayed by the crop duster?"

"I'm just lucky, I guess," I said.

"Uncle Allen was quite a hero tonight," Angie told me. "He ran out in the field while the crop duster was still spraying and carried you back to his truck. He hosed you off and raced you to the hospital, and then called Mr. Grant to bring us. He thought you'd want us to be here when you woke up. He doesn't seem like such a mean man after all."

Jeremy found the remote control to the television and turned it on. He flipped through all the channels, but they were all just snow and hissing—you couldn't make out a single thing on any of them.

"Now I don't feel so bad," he said to me with a grin. "You're going to be just as bored as we are."

"Are you kidding?" Angie said. "He's got a lot of reading to do. He's got to finish what he started." She unzipped her backpack again and reached inside.

"Oh no!" I said. "I don't ever want to see that UFO magazine again. Just throw it away!"

Angie grinned and pulled her Bible out of the

backpack. "Wrong again!" she said and handed me the Bible.

I held it in my hands a moment, then I opened it and flipped through the pages. It was well worn and had a lot of writing in the margins.

"Thank you," I told her, smiling. "I *do* have a lot of reading to do."

Don't miss another exciting

HEEBIE JEEBIES

adventure!

Turn the page to check out chapters from

THE MYSTERIOUS TREASURE
OF THE SLIMY SEA CAVE

Chapter 1

Skin diving in the dark? Why me? I must be nuts. Either that or I'm in the mood for night swimming with sharks—which I guess would mean I'm nuts.

As the waves crumble past my snorkel, I try to figure out what brought me here. Then I notice the abalone iron in my right hand. It's a foot long and flat like a small crowbar, the perfect tool for prying. That explains it. I'm hunting abalone, my Gram's favorite food. We can't afford to buy it in the store.

But why at night? Lobsters come out after dark, but not abalone. And why is everything so blurry? I lift my head out of the water and wipe both sides of my mask. Still bad. Nothing is in focus.

Oh well, I'll just have to tough it out. Swimming forward, I hover along the surface of the choppy sea. The flashlight in my left hand slices through the water like a white laser. Moving it from side to side, I eye the bottom of the reef. From above, abalone look like giant clams, with one difference. Clams have two half-shells that close together. Abalone only have half a shell. The open underside has a giant muscle that clings to the rocks, which explains the need for an iron bar to pry them loose. The muscle is what you eat.

Kicking ahead with my fins, I keep watch for my prey. A milky haze hangs in the water just outside the flashlight's beam. Strands of kelp rise from the ocean floor and sway like willow trees in the wind. A few perch swim by, but otherwise the ocean is deserted, almost as if a sea monster has scared everything off.

If I swim just a little farther, I'll be at the cliffs north of town. The water is shallow there and filled with boulders, creating the perfect abalone habitat.

A loud bark catches my attention. Lifting my head, I quickly scan the surrounding sea in the pale moonlight. About fifty feet away, high atop Bride Rock, a sea lion is glaring at me.

He roars again. "What's the problem?" I mumble into my snorkel.

Suddenly a massive wave sloshes around Bride Rock and rolls straight toward me. Gulping down a mouthful of air, I dive deep, waiting for the white wash to tumble overhead.

Caught in the beam from my flashlight, I notice what has to be the world's largest abalone. Clinging to a boulder about fifteen feet below, its shell sparkles like black gold. Talk about buried treasure! The longer I look, the more I have to have it. Rising to the surface, I take several deep breaths and plot my attack. At that depth, I can hold my breath for a minute, max, before having to rise.

I'm hungry, but hesitant. My attack must be quick and precise. I must quickly slip the iron bar underneath the abalone's shell and pop the giant loose. If I don't pull it off in one swift motion, the abalone will get spooked and clamp down tight. Once that happens, I'll never pry it loose.

Doubling over, I position my fins above me and kick like a seal. My heart pounds against my ribs as I descend through the dark and murky water. With my hand just a few inches from the shell, I slide my iron under it and twist. In a flash, my iron pops free. But the abalone is gone! I jab at the rock and barnacles. How could an abalone simply disappear? It doesn't make sense.

My air is running out, but I search desperately, unwilling to give up. My eyes bulge in my dive mask. I have to surface, but something strange is keeping me here—a dark desire to gain the treasure no matter what. I scrape and dig, held down by a new, stubborn greed.

Finally, I concede defeat and attempt to rise. But my abalone iron won't slide free. I yank and heave in a nautical tug-of-war, but the iron bar feels like it is under an elephant's foot. I have to leave it behind. Letting go, I kick for the surface.

Wham!

My head collides with a ceiling of barnacles on a rock that hovers over me. Where did that come from? Swimming beneath the jagged slab, I search for an opening. My lungs want to collapse. My fingers tingle from lack of oxygen. I thrash through the water on the brink of drowning. Suddenly, walls appear on both sides of me, forming a sea cave. The more I swim, the more entombed I become.

Something green slithers past me. I turn just as a serpent's tail disappears into the darkness. I raise my fists in defense, but it doesn't return.

The sea cave begins to shake and rumble as if in the stomach of a volcano. Crabs drop from the rocks, unable to hold on. Kelp are torn from their roots. Debris and sand cloud the water. I can't see anything, and I can't hold my breath any longer.

I feel like I'm in a blender. I can't fight it any-more and begin to black out. My lungs are ready to burst and take my heart with them. The rumbling intensifies.

Then something grabs my arm. It must be the serpent, back to chomp me to pieces.

"Nate!" a voice calls.

The turbulence around me continues.

"Nate!" the voice repeats, sounding more famil-iar. "Wake up!"

The outline of a woman's face peers down at me. It's Gram. But she doesn't go skin diving. What's going on?

"Get up! Quick!" She hollers, pulling me by the arm. "It's an earthquake!"

Sitting up in bed, I realize what has happened. I've gone from one nightmare to another. But this one is real. The sea cave doesn't exist, but the earthquake does, and our old house is about to come crashing down.

Tossing my covers aside, I scrambled under my desk. Gram made her way to the door frame and stood under it.

"Where's Paige?" I asked.

"What?" Gram hollered, unable to hear me over the rumbling.

This time I yelled. "I said, where's Paige?"

"She's already under her desk. She's fine."

As the earthquake intensified, I wondered whether our house would survive. The windows rattled almost to the point of shattering. Pictures on the walls swung like pendulums. The crash of glass breaking echoed from the kitchen.

Closing my eyes, I prayed for God to keep us safe. I also asked Him to watch over our house. I knew Gram didn't have earthquake insurance, or, for that matter, any money for repairs.

Huddling under my desk, I marvelled at the night's events. To have such a vivid and eerie dream followed by a real earthquake was too bizarre to be a coincidence. As the shaking subsided, I tried to make sense of it all; but nothing I imagined came close to what would soon unfold in the wake of this ominous night.

Chapter 2

The next morning Paige and I helped Gram clean up. Miraculously, the tremor had only broken two glasses, so it didn't take long. I checked outside and found no further damage. We all exhaled in relief.

"Looks like God answered my prayer," I said.

"He always does," Gram added with a smile. She has blonde hair with a touch of gray. People always say she looks too young to be a grandma.

Following a quick cereal breakfast, I headed for the phone to call Zack, my best friend. He's in ninth grade like I am and always ready for an adventure. But as I reached for the receiver, I hesitated. After last night's dream, I wasn't as excited about our plans to go skin diving. Then again, that was only a dream. There isn't a sea cave anywhere near Starboard, which is where I live.

Finally, the thought of abalone for dinner was too tempting to pass up. I picked up the phone and dialed Zack's number.

"How's the house, Dude?" he asked me right away.

"A few glasses broke, but that's it," I told him.

"Same here."

"So are you ready?" I asked, eager to change the subject.

"For what?"

"Skin diving. It's ocean time."

"Not for me. I've got plans to go treasure hunting."

If treasure hunting meant searching for buried treasure in the sea, I would jump at the chance to go along. But it doesn't. For Zack, treasure hunting means garage sales. He collects artifacts and antiques related to the ocean. Because some of the houses in Starboard are over 100 years old, garage sales provide the best and most affordable way to feed his addiction. Some of his finds include a harpoon, a pirate's sword, a brass bell, a compass, a cannon ball, and a captain's log dating from the 1880s. He has lots of other stuff too, some of which is kind of cool, but hardly worth living for.

"How do you know if there are any garage sales today?" I asked, hoping to persuade him to come along.

"My mom saw a sign when she went for her morning walk. Let's skin dive when I get back."

"The water will be choppy by then. Why don't you hit the garage sale later?"

Zack snorted. "All the good stuff will be gone. You know that."

I did but figured it was worth a try. When neither of us would give in, we agreed to go our separate ways.

"I'll go with you," Paige called from the other room.

Before I could answer, she came clomping around the corner, already decked out in her bright pink wetsuit with matching fins, snorkel, and mask. Her long, blonde hair was pulled back in a ponytail. At eleven years old, Paige is small for her age, but that doesn't hamper her ability in the ocean. My sister not only looks like a mermaid, she swims like one.

"I'll go with you," she repeated.

"Nah, that's ok," I said, feeling some relief that it wasn't going to work out. As hard as I tried, I just couldn't get the sea cave nightmare out of my mind.

"Come on," Paige persisted. "You know how much an abalone dinner would mean to Gram, especially after losing two glasses and her favorite vase."

"Her favorite vase?"

Paige nodded. "All it did was fall over, but that was enough to crack the crystal."

I felt terrible because I knew that the vase could not be replaced. What little money Gram earns goes to supporting Paige and me. When I was three and Paige was one, our parents died at sea during a storm that capsized their boat. Gram was our only living relative, so we came to stay with her. Even though we cramp her living space and she has to give up so much of what she enjoys, she never complains. Instead, she carries on about how blessed she is to raise us as her own.

"You're sure you want to go?" I asked, stalling. "The earthquake might have churned up the water pretty good. Maybe some kind of slimy sea monster was released from the deep."

Paige scrunched her eyebrows together. "Yeah, sure. A sea monster. Let's go."

I watched as Gram carefully laid the vase in the trash and closed the lid. Keeping her face hidden from us, she walked down the hall to her bedroom. That was enough for me.

"All right," I said. "Let's go catch some dinner for Gram." As the words crossed my lips, all I could think about was the green tail of a serpent wrapped around my throat and holding me down.

More exciting releases from

More exciting releases from

THE NEW QUICK-READING TALES THAT ENTERTAIN WHILE AFFIRMING THE PRESENCE AND POWER OF GOD!

In this eerie tale filled with unexpected thrills and chills, Heather and Todd pursue an investigation to learn about a mysterious abandoned camp, their father's own secret involvement, and God's all-powerful protection and love.

Welcome to Camp Creeps
0-8054-1195-X

Twelve-year-old Daniel finds himself face-to-face with a ten-foot long rat and his own guilty conscience in the first edition of the spine-chilling *Heebie Jeebies* series. Will Daniel learn that covering up a mistake can be the biggest mistake of all?

The Rat That Ate Poodles
0-8054-0170-9

available at fine bookstores everywhere